The Practice Kiss

1

As I stumbled through the neon-lit back streets of Seoul, I wondered whether I'd freeze to death if I had to sleep outside tonight.

My tired arms dragged my heavy suitcase over the rough pavement, the dizzyingly bright, colourful storefronts and signs becoming a blur as my head spun, drunk from the soju. I tried to focus, desperately grasping for some kind of solution.

I'd spent the last year dreaming and preparing for this… How could it all have gone so terribly wrong? *Should I call my parents and admit defeat? I couldn't even make it 24 hours…*I swallowed dryly, an uncomfortable lump in my throat.

Salty, spicy, pungent fumes drifted from the doorways of restaurants into the night air. My stomach lurched. In a haze of nausea, I staggered forward, hunger and exhaustion stabbing my body.

I stopped outside a convenience store and fumbled in my jeans pocket, retrieving my phone. I stared in disbelief at the low-battery warning displayed on the screen. Overcome with hopelessness, my eyes filled up with tears. I dropped to the ground feeling dizzy and lost, unable to think straight or to ask for help. Hurried passersby ignored my crumpled figure. Under the glow of a flickering, buzzing fluorescent sign, I leaned my head against my suitcase. *I give up.*

2

Eight hours earlier

I burst through the arrivals gate at Incheon International Airport, brimming with excitement. *Today, my new life begins as an English teacher in South Korea.*

With a deep breath, I stepped forward, wheeling my suitcase over the shiny, tiled floor. Friends, relatives, and colleagues of arriving travellers gathered behind the barrier rails, a buzz of anticipation in the air.

The teacher placement agency, SK-Teach, had booked and pre-paid a driver to pick me up and take me to my accommodation—a studio apartment that the school was providing for me. I scanned the crowd, searching for someone holding a sign with my name on it.

Searching…searching…

Hmmm. No "Chloe Gibson" sign in sight. *How odd.* I had been assured that there would be someone to meet me at the gate.

I stood and waited a while longer, but fatigue quickly

caught up with me. I hadn't slept on the flight. My ears were blocked, and my head was foggy. It felt like I was underwater. I moved to a nearby row of chairs, where I slumped down, suitcase in front of me and backpack on my lap.

I pulled my phone out from my jacket pocket. Using the free airport WiFi, I checked my emails in case I had been sent updated plans. Scrolling through my inbox revealed nothing but junk mail. I sighed heavily. Resting my head in my hands, I continued to watch the small gathering around the gate.

Several batches of arrivals came and went. At last, I conceded that no one was coming to pick me up. There must have been some kind of mix-up.

I'll just take a taxi, I decided, certain that I could be reimbursed for the fare. Before leaving the terminal, I called my contact at SK-Teach. An automated message played: "The number you have called is not available." *Gah*. I composed a short email instead, letting them know that I was leaving the airport.

As soon as I pressed send, I headed out the airport doors and into the fresh afternoon air. I spotted the rank of bright orange taxis immediately. I waved to the driver first in queue. He got out of the car.

"Good afternoon," he said in English.

"Afternoon," I replied.

He hauled my suitcase and backpack into the boot, then opened the door for me. I made myself comfortable in the back seat. The taxi was clean and smelled as if it had been freshly filled with petrol.

"Where are you going today?" the driver asked.

I handed him a printout of the location of my apartment in Mapo-gu, Seoul.

"First time in Korea?" the driver asked, pulling out from the rank.

"No. I lived here for a year when I was sixteen. I did a high school exchange trip."

"Wow. You must have been outgoing to do that at such a young age."

"It was hard at first, but my host family was so kind and welcoming."

"Can you speak Korean?"

"Yes."

"Oh, that's good."

I gazed out the window, watching the cars go by on the expressway—Kias and Hyundais in white, silver, and black. The driving style looked chaotic, with cars weaving in and out of lanes without indicating. This didn't faze the taxi driver, who engaged in the same behaviour himself.

"What brings you back to Korea?" he asked.

"I've been hired as an English teacher."

"Ah, I see. Lots of foreigners come here to do that."

The overcast sky lent a dreary atmosphere to the city and the monotonous view from the expressway caused me to yawn. I closed my eyes, only meaning to rest them temporarily, but when I opened them again, we were in the heart of Seoul.

I snapped upright, absorbing the sights and sounds of the bustling metropolis around me, a jumbled mixture of high-tech, futuristic skyscrapers, plus older, low-rise buildings, some of them rundown and dilapidated.

The streets hummed with activity, hordes of people walking the footpaths, past shops, restaurants, offices, and street food vendors.

We continued to drive, winding through side streets as the last rays of afternoon sunlight pierced a gap in the clouds.

Eventually we came to a residential neighbourhood composed mainly of houses and apartment blocks. There were fewer cars and people around. Grassy areas provided a more relaxed, suburban feel.

The car slowed, then pulled over. "Rose Tower" read the sign on the building up ahead. I recognised it from the pictures I had been sent. Around 20 floors high and with a peachy-pink exterior. A small courtyard and garden bordered its entrance.

"The fare is 62,000 won," the driver said.

"I'll pay by credit card."

He passed me the card reader and I inserted my credit card. An error message appeared on the screen. I tried again but it still didn't work.

"It's not working for some reason," I said. "I'll pay cash." I counted my money and offloaded a wad of notes, leaving my wallet considerably lighter.

"Thank you."

We got out of the car and he retrieved my luggage from the boot.

"Enjoy your time in Korea." He bowed.

"Thanks!"

Excited to finally get settled in my apartment, I crossed the road and approached the building. Glass double doors marked the entrance to the lobby. Raising a shaky hand, I reached out and pushed the door…but it wouldn't open. I tried to pull instead, but that didn't work either. *Hmmm…Is there something I need to press?* I noticed a panel at the side of the door and some kind of sensor. *Ah! I must need an access card to get in. How inconvenient.* I hadn't been told about this, and I hadn't been provided with one. Frustrated, I set my luggage down and took out my phone. I tried to call SK-Teach again.

"The number you have called is not available."

Is my phone not working? Maybe I should have bought a new sim card at the airport…

I checked my emails. A new message appeared at the top of my inbox, subject line: Message delivery failed. Clicking the email, I saw that the earlier message I sent had bounced. A deep unease unfurled in my stomach. *What's going on? Why can't I contact the agency?*

I took a few deep breaths to calm myself. It's okay, I assured myself. It was a big building. It wouldn't be long before a resident would come and open the door, and I could follow them in. I sat down on the edge of a planter box near the entry and assumed stake-out mode.

As time passed, I grew increasingly drowsy. I could barely keep my eyes open. *Please…someone come soon…*

Finally, my ears pricked at the sound of footsteps approaching. I sprang into action, swiftly moving in behind the female resident. She opened the door, and I followed her inside. The door swung closed behind me and locked with a clunk. I exhaled in relief. *I'm in.*

The small, plain lobby had white walls, a tiled floor, and three elevators. I followed the woman into the middle elevator. She swiped her access card and pressed six. I pushed ten, but it didn't activate without a card. The woman gave me a questioning look and I mumbled something about losing my card by way of explanation.

After the short ride up, the elevator doors opened at the sixth floor and the woman departed. I had no choice but to get out and take the stairs the rest of the way.

The windowless corridor was dark and narrow. I followed

an illuminated green sign to the fire exit and pushed open the door. The steep flight of stairs rose up in front of me like a mountain. I groaned inwardly. Gathering all my strength, I lugged my suitcase up the staircase, step by agonising step.

By the time I reached the tenth floor, my arms ached and sweat soaked my top. I burst out into the corridor, gasping for breath.

As soon as I had recovered, I scanned the row of doors for my apartment number—10F.

There it is. I stood in front of the door to my apartment, almost crying with relief. Now, the only obstacle in my way was the digital lock. Luckily, I knew the code and had already memorised it off by heart. I reached for the keypad and typed the number in. 4910.

Nothing happened.

Did I type it wrong? I tried again.

Nope, still didn't work.

I groped in my backpack for my wallet, where I had stowed a slip of paper with the door code. I double checked it. *4910.* My heart dropped. *Something is seriously wrong here.*

Out of desperation, I knocked on the door. I heard movement in the apartment. A strange old man opened the door and looked at me with a surprised expression on his face.

"What is this?" he asked in Korean.

"Sorry! Wrong apartment!"

Flustered, I hurried away.

My head reeled. *What's going on? What should I do?*

I took the elevator back down to the lobby.

This must be a mistake…

Once again, I tried to contact SK-Teach. No luck.

Changing tack, I decided to call the school instead. *They might know what's going on.* I hadn't dealt with the school directly since my interview with the principal. I had to look up the school's phone number. I paced backwards and forwards as the phone rang, willing someone to pick up.

"Hello, this is Gongwon School reception."

"Yes, hello. My name is Chloe Gibson. I'm the new English teacher. I need to speak to Principal Choi."

"Chloe…Gibson…?"

"That's right."

"I can't find your name on our staff list."

"Maybe it hasn't been added yet?"

"That shouldn't be the case…Hold on. I will ask Principal Choi."

She put me on hold. My stomach undulated with nerves as I waited. *Principal Choi knows me. He should be able to sort out this mess…*

Eventually, she picked back up.

"I'm sorry. Principal Choi has not heard of you. There hasn't been a new English teacher hired this year."

My world came crashing down as reality hit me.

3

T he pieces slowly drifted into place. *It was all a scam.* The interview must have been fake. The job contract and the apartment lease too.

I felt sick to the pit of my stomach, frozen in shock, unable to move, unable to think straight. Completely numb.

I stood in a state of stupor until the elevator door suddenly opened, startling me. The young man who walked out threw me a curious glance but continued on his way.

I can't stay here. It was already dark outside. I needed to find a place to stay the night. I could decide what to do after a good, long sleep.

I checked Kakao Maps for the nearest hotel. Only a fifteen-minute walk away, but I couldn't bear to drag my suitcase that far. Instead, I walked to the nearest main street and hailed a taxi. A grey-coloured cab pulled over. The driver flung my luggage in the boot and I hopped in the back seat.

"Crane Hotel, please," I said.

A short drive later we arrived at the hotel. I paid the small fare with cash.

Standing outside the hotel, the rapid beat of my heart stabilised. I felt safe in the knowledge I would soon be resting in a warm and comfortable hotel room.

Warm light emanated from the hotel windows, inviting me inside. I stepped through the revolving door into a stylish, contemporary lobby, with a polished concrete floor, and plush, designer furniture. I approached the reception desk where a woman wearing a navy-blue suit and a silk scarf around her neck talked on the phone. When her lengthy conversation concluded, she finally turned her attention to me.

"Hello. How can I help you?" she asked in English.

"I'd like to check in. I don't have a room booked…"

"I see." She looked at her computer screen. "We have standard and deluxe rooms available."

"Standard is fine."

"How many nights?"

"Just one, for now."

The woman printed out a form. She handed it to me, along with a pen. "Please fill in your details."

I quickly scrawled down my information and slid the form back to her across the desk.

"Perfect." She took the form. "Now, I just need you credit card to confirm the booking."

I fished it out of my wallet. "Here you go."

She inserted my card and prompted me to enter my PIN on the keypad.

Processing…

Transaction declined.

I remembered how the card hadn't worked in the airport taxi either. "Sorry. Let me try a different card."

I used my debit card but received the same message. I started to sweat. *Why aren't my cards working?*

"I don't know what's wrong," I stammered. "Can I pay in cash?"

The woman shook her head. "We need a card on file to cover incidentals."

"Please? I really need to book this room."

"I'm sorry. Our system can't process the booking without a card. There's nothing I can do."

"I see…Then I'll have to go somewhere else."

Head hung low, I retreated from the desk. My body trembled with accumulated frustration and exhaustion. I sat down on a chair in the lobby and wearily opened my banking app. When the app loaded, my heart jumped in shock. My account balance showed I was in overdraft and my credit card was maxed out. *What the hell?*

I scrolled through the transactions, my hand shaking. Large withdrawals had been made from my account, all of them during the timeframe I had been on the plane.

Not only had my teaching placement been a scam, but they had also taken my money.

Freaking out, I called my bank. Music played as I waited in the hold queue.

"Your wait time is approximately 45 minutes," played an automated message.

"45 minutes!" I repeated in disbelief.

Sighing, I curled up on the chair and closed my eyes, phone pressed to my ear. The same song played over and over again until its tune was drilled into my brain.

I was practically dead by the time I was finally put through to a customer service representative.

"How can I help you today?" he asked, cheerily.

I blurted out my situation and he quickly cancelled my cards and filed a fraud report.

"We should be able to get these transactions reversed, but it could take a few days…" he explained.

"When will I be able to get new cards sent to me? I'm in South Korea right now."

"South Korea? I'll arrange express international delivery. Where are you staying?"

"Uh…actually…I don't have an address right now. I'll have to get back to you."

He gave me his direct line so I could call him back.

Ending the phone call, I realised my dilemma was only partially resolved. I should be able to get my money back and a new card, but for now I would somehow have to survive on the limited amount of cash I had left.

I counted my money. 103,000 won. That would have to pay for food and accommodation and whatever else I needed, possibly for a few days. Where could I stay that would accept cash and not cost too much? A hostel dorm? A *jjimjilbbang*?

Across the room at the lobby bar, two businessmen sat drinking beers and eating fried chicken. My stomach growled with a sharp stab of hunger. I hadn't eaten in hours. *I need food*…It would be easier to think about what to do with a full stomach.

I heaved myself up to venture outside. A blast of freezing air slammed into me as I stumbled out the door and I tightened my scarf, huddling closer into its warmth. My breath came out in puffs of mist as I walked the moonlit street, searching for a place to eat.

I halted when the delicious smell of fried food tugged at my nostrils. I followed a trail of wafting steam to a *pojangmacha* —rows of orange tents with transparent plastic windows, through which I could see tables and chairs, people, and a bar laden with trays of food.

The sound of meat sizzling, broth bubbling, and people chatting pulled me closer. Shivering, I entered the tent. Heaters inside provided immediate comfort.

I took a seat at the bar and ordered *tteokbokki* and soju. Speaking in fluent Korean was enough to deter the vendor from attempting to rip me off with inflated tourist prices, despite the enormous suitcase by my side.

The food and soju were promptly served, and I snapped apart a pair of disposable chopsticks. I popped one of the cylindrical rice cakes into my mouth, then another, and another. I ate too fast, launching a coughing fit. The dark red broth overpowered my weak stomach.

While I waited for my stomach to settle, I poured a glass of soju. I drank it in one gulp. The strong, slightly sweet, clear liquid warmed my throat.

I continued to drink while turning over my situation in my head. I could find a place to stay the night, but then what? Search for another teaching position at this late stage? Contact my old host family and ask them for help? Just give up and call my parents and ask them to book me on the next flight home?

I downed another shot of soju. My parents had been against me going to Korea in the first place. The thought of telling them I had failed was unbearable.

Asking my host family for help wasn't palatable either. They were poor and lived all the way in Tongyeong. I didn't wish to burden them.

No closer to a resolution, I drank until my worries numbed. I tried to eat more food, but my stomach rejected it despite my hunger. My head felt heavy. How I wished to lay it on a soft pillow…I had to peel my eyes open to keep myself from falling asleep at the bar. I hopped down, leaving the empty soju bottle and my half-finished meal.

Towing my suitcase behind me, I set out, stumbling along the back streets of Seoul. My head spun, and the bright, colourfully lit streets became a blur as I walked.

I willed myself to focus, but I couldn't.

I stopped outside a convenience store and took out my phone. The screen displayed a low-battery warning.

At that point, I lost it. I dropped to the ground, crying. *I give up.*

I'd have to call my parents and ask to come home. The thought made me wail even louder.

"Hello? Are you all right?" a female voice asked in Korean.

I looked up, wiping away tears.

A woman in corporate attire and her hair pulled back in a low ponytail stood watching me.

"No. I'm not all right. Everything has gone wrong," I replied.

The woman looked surprised. "You speak Korean well." She offered me her hand and pulled me up. "My name is Seo Minjung. I work for KAM Entertainment." She passed me her business card.

Seo Minjung
Talent Recruitment Executive
KAM Entertainment, Gangnam, Seoul

"I think I can help you," she said.

A wave of relief swept over me.

She took me to a nearby café. The dimly lit room was divided into comfy booths containing worn, brown couches and wooden tables. Shelves messily crammed with old books separated the booths. The air smelled of fresh coffee, chocolate, and pastry.

"Let me buy you something to eat and drink," Minjung said, approaching the counter.

"I'm fine," I stammered, taken aback by her kindness to a stranger she just met on the street.

Minjung scrutinised me, unconvinced. "No, you're not. Come on. What would you like to drink?"

"My stomach is a bit upset…" I clutched it tenderly.

"How about a chamomile tea? It's good for settling a sore stomach."

"Hmmm…That sounds nice."

Minjung ordered and then we sat down in one of the booths. She looked at me with concern, her big, round eyes sympathetic. "So…what's your story?"

My head continued to spin. I took a big breath to calm myself before answering. "I arrived in Seoul today to start an English teaching job…but it turned out the job didn't exist."

"Why is that?"

"I was scammed by a sham recruitment company."

Minjung gasped. "*Omo*…"

"The apartment lease they arranged was fake as well. They also took my money."

"So that's what happened. No wonder you were so upset."

"I don't have anywhere to stay. All I have is around 100,000 won in cash."

Minjung chewed her lip. "I see. You're in a tough predicament."

I nodded, wearily.

A girl in a black apron served us—a chamomile tea for me, an Americano for Minjung.

"Drink up," Minjung said.

I took a calming sip.

Minjung cradled her coffee cup, a thoughtful expression on her face. "Chloe…I think I can help."

"Really?"

She nodded. "But I have a proposal for you."

So, there's a catch…

"Okay. What is it?"

"Do you have any acting experience?"

4

"Acting experience?" I repeated, bemused.

"Yes. Do you?" Minjung pressed.

"Well, I've been in school productions…I took drama lessons throughout high school too."

"That's something!"

"Why do you want to know?"

"The truth is, I had a motive for approaching you on the street…"

"Oh?"

"When I saw you, I thought you would be the perfect fit for a role."

"An acting role?"

"That's right. On a drama."

My mouth dropped open. "Me? Appear in a drama?"

"Exactly."

I couldn't believe what I was hearing. This couldn't be right, could it? It must be the alcohol, the exhaustion…*I'm delirious.*

I took her business card out of my pocket and looked at it

again, focusing my blurry vision. "You work for KAM Entertainment."

"That's right. We specialise in sourcing and developing actors and models. There's a new drama due to begin filming on Thursday, but one of the actors pulled out at the last minute. There's been a desperate rush to fill her role."

"And you think I would suit the role?"

Minjung nodded. "A good-looking foreigner who can speak Korean fluently. You even resemble her. You're about the same size too, so wardrobe shouldn't need to make many adjustments…"

Is this real? Am I dreaming?

"Is this something you would be interested in?" Minjung asked.

My heart raced. "Are you kidding? It would be a dream come true!"

"Great! You'll still need to audition, of course. But it's a minor role, and at this late stage, I don't think they're going to be too picky."

I felt dizzy with excitement and disbelief.

Minjung continued. "I'll take you to KAM tomorrow and arrange a meeting with the director. As for tonight…I can't offer much, but I do have a couch you can sleep on. Would that be all right?"

Under normal circumstances I wouldn't go and sleep in a stranger's house, but these weren't normal circumstances, and what other option did I have?

"Yes. Thank you!"

I hastily slurped back my tea.

"Are you ready to go? It's a quick ride on the subway to my place," Minjung said.

I nodded. "Let's go."

We ditched the cozy café for the bitter cold street. Minjung pulled my suitcase for me, a relief to my aching arms. She led the way to the nearest subway entrance.

We entered a large station, bustling with workers heading home after a long day at the office. Through turnstiles and down an escalator, we reached the platform. The train had already arrived, and we managed to board just before the doors closed.

It was a short journey to Hapjeong station. From the exit, we emerged on a busy main street lined with shops and high-rise towers.

I followed Minjung down back roads with a quainter vibe, past coffee shops and small apartment buildings. We stopped outside a nondescript building the colour of concrete. She unlocked the door and let me in.

Minjung's apartment was on the third floor. She entered her passcode and pushed open the door.

"I'm home!" she said, taking off her shoes at the entrance.

The compact apartment had white walls and a wooden floor, with house plants, cushions, and art prints providing pops of colour to the otherwise minimalist interior.

A man sat at a small table by the window, a book in one hand and a coffee cup in the other. He lifted his head and peered at us through his thick glasses. "You're home late. Who's that?"

"Potential new talent."

"My name's Chloe," I said, removing my shoes.

"I'm Gong Dongsik, Minjung's husband."

"She'll be sleeping here tonight," Minjung stated.

Dongsik raised his eyebrows at this news but didn't push back.

"Sorry to intrude," I said.

"Sit down," Minjung said. "You must be so tired."

I made myself comfortable on the couch.

Minjung rummaged in a closet and retrieved a warm blanket and a pillow. She passed them to me.

"Thank you," I said.

"Feel free to have a shower. And help yourself to anything in the kitchen."

"Hmmm…I might use the shower." Although I was eager to go to sleep, I was more desperate to wash off the layer of grime which had accumulated on my skin and in my hair.

"Of course. Oh, but before that, can I take a couple photos of you? I want to send them to Mr. Kim at KAM. I'm sure he'll be very pleased that I found you."

"Okay. I don't look my best, though…" I ran my fingers through my messy hair, trying to comb it.

"You look fine," Minjung assured me. "Stand here."

I stood in front of the white wall.

Minjung snapped two pictures of me with her phone—one close-up and one full-length shot.

"There. You can go and have your shower now. I'll let you know what Mr. Kim says."

I grabbed my toiletries bag and a pair of pyjamas from my suitcase before heading to the bathroom. Minjung tossed me a clean towel on my way.

I quickly undressed and got in the shower. The hot water felt amazing on my bare skin. My aching muscles sighed with relief. *I've had the strangest day*, I reflected as the water flowed over me.

One year ago, I quit a soul-destroying job and moved back in with my parents. Depressed, I spent my days binge-watching K-dramas, not knowing what to do with my life. Eventually, those K-dramas gave me the idea to go to Korea and teach English. And now, I actually had the chance to *be in* a K-drama. Nothing could make me happier.

After scrubbing myself from head to toe, I emerged feeling thoroughly cleansed and refreshed. I put my pyjamas on and wrapped my hair in the towel.

As I left the bathroom, Minjung's phone started to ring.

"It's Mr. Kim!" she said.

Butterflies in my stomach, I listened as she answered the call.

5

"He wants to meet you first thing tomorrow!" Minjung said excitedly when she had finished talking with Mr. Kim.

"That sounds promising," Dongsik said. "Is it for the part in Hidden History?"

"Yes."

"Should I do anything to prepare?" I asked.

Minjung shook her head. "Just try to have a good sleep. There will be time to look over the script tomorrow. We'll leave you to get some rest."

"Goodnight," Dongsik said.

They retreated to their bedroom.

Alone in the dark room, I lay on the couch and pulled the blanket over me. Thoughts swirled in my head, becoming more and more nonsensical until they turned into dreams. I slept heavily through the night.

In the morning, the smell of breakfast prompted me to open my eyes. Minjung prepared kimchi, rice, and soup. I sat up and breathed in the powerful aromas.

"Oh, you're awake," Minjung said.

"Do you need any help?" I asked, stifling a yawn.

"No. I'm just reheating leftovers."

"Morning," Dongsik said, emerging from the bedroom. He wore a dark grey suit and a striped tie. "Sleep well?"

"I did. This couch is comfortable."

"That's good to hear. Come and join us for breakfast when you're ready."

I got changed in the bathroom, then sat down with Minjung and Dongsik at the table.

"Looks delicious," I said.

Minjung shrugged. "It's nothing much."

I wolfed down the food, my stomach having fully recovered from the previous night.

"Ah! Look at the time," Minjung said. "We'd better get going."

"I can drop you off at the station," Dongsik said.

In a flurry, we got ready to leave.

"Let's go." Dongsik rallied us out the door.

We descended the stairs to an underground carpark where Dongsik unlocked a white SUV. I hopped in the back seat.

Early morning sunlight poured in as we surfaced from the carpark. Commuters in business attire crowded the roads and paths.

After a short drive, Dongsik pulled over near the subway entrance. "*Hwaiting*! I'm rooting for you."

"Thank you!"

We hopped out and Dongsik drove away.

I stayed glued to Minjung's side in the jam-packed subway station, terrified that we'd get separated as people pushed and shoved their way around us. Eventually, we managed to squish ourselves into a train carriage.

An uncomfortable forty-minute ride to Gangnam Station ensued. I sighed with relief when we finally made it.

In trendy central Gangnam, Minjung guided the way to the KAM building.

"Here we are," she said at last.

The large office building had light grey panelled walls and a border of planter boxes providing pretty greenery. A discreet plaque by the entrance read "KAM Entertainment."

Minjung swiped her employee ID to enter and I followed her in.

"Whoa," I said, looking around as we entered a spacious and modern reception area. Large screens displayed a rotation of glamorous shots of the talent. *They're gorgeous…I wonder if I'll get to meet any of them.* I stood transfixed until Minjung tore me away.

"We're going to Mr. Kim's office on the fifth floor." She steered me towards the elevators.

When we reached the fifth floor, the elevator doors opened to reveal a posh suite of executive offices. We walked into Mr. Kim's office. He stood up from his desk when we approached. Despite his age, he looked trendy, wearing a plain, white t-shirt under a blue blazer.

"You must be Chloe Gibson." He grinned enthusiastically.

"Yes, Mr. Kim," I said.

"Please, take a seat." He motioned to the leather couch at the side of the room.

"I'll leave you to it." Minjung flashed me a look of encouragement before slipping away.

I sat down. Mr. Kim pulled up his chair to sit opposite me.

"Now, as I'm sure Minjung explained to you, there is an urgent role to fill on the drama Hidden History. It's not a lead part, but it's crucial to the storyline, that's why the character can't simply be written out."

He reached over to his desk and picked up a comb-bound document. He tossed it into my lap.

Hidden History
Episode 1 script

"The character is Louise Sullivan. She's the only foreigner in the small town. She works at a bar and attracts a lot of customers due to their curiosity. Louise seems, how should I say this…*ditzy* at first. But it's an act. She's actually an under-cover reporter for a foreign newspaper. In fact, Louise Sullivan isn't even her real name. She's in town to investigate a cold case—a string of disappearances, which seem somehow linked with her Korean friend back in the UK. Early in the series, Louise ends up dead."

"She found out too much?"

Mr. Kim snapped his fingers. "You've got it."

"She sounds like an interesting character."

"Right? An actress called Tamara Wilson had been cast to play her, but the poor thing found out her father's terminally ill. She pulled out so she could go back to England to be with him."

Mr. Kim pulled out his phone and brought up a photo. He showed it to me. "This is Tamara."

The woman looked to be in her mid-twenties, fair and blonde, with hazel eyes. I realised why I had caught Minjung's attention on the street. I looked just like Tamara.

"The resemblance is amazing, isn't it? I feel like you could slip right into her place. As long as you can act reasonably well, I don't think the director would hesitate to cast you. Minjung told me you've been in plays?"

"That's right."

Never in a lead role, though…

"The programme director, Im Nara, is coming in—" Mr. Kim checked his watch, "—just over an hour. She'll audition you. In the meantime, I want you to practice your lines from the first episode. There aren't too many."

"Okay." I clutched the script in my sweaty hands, suddenly feeling the pressure.

"I think Minjung has booked a practice room for you." Mr. Kim stood up. "Come with me."

I followed him to an open-plan area with rows of cubicles. Minjung sat at a desk overflowing with files.

"Seo Minjung-ssi, take Chloe to a practice room. Better send an intern as well."

"Yes, Mr. Kim."

"Chloe, we'll speak again if you pass the audition. Good luck."

I nodded. "Thank you, Mr. Kim."

He left me with Minjung.

One hour to learn my lines. I felt jittery all over, my insides twisting and turning with nerves.

"Are you ready?" Minjung asked.

I hesitated. "Uh, I need to use the bathroom…"

"Of course. It's down that corridor, on the left."

"Thanks. I'll be right back."

My thoughts swirled as I walked towards the bathroom. *What if I don't pass the audition? What if I end up back where I started—homeless and jobless?* I pushed open the bathroom door in a daze. *What's this?* A row of urinals. A man with a shocked expression on his face. *Oh crap.*

6

The tall young man wore a denim shirt and slim black jeans. He had a mop of wavy, dark brown hair. Under straight eyebrows, two bright, smiley eyes, squishy cheeks, and a broad mouth.

So cute…I wonder if he's talent?

He looked at me with an expression of bewilderment on his face. I snapped to my senses.

"Sorry!" I stammered, before running out with my arms flailing.

In the safety of the women's bathroom, I took deep breaths and fanned myself with my hands.

"Calm down," I said to myself in the mirror.

I couldn't let an accidental detour into the men's bathroom faze me. I needed to focus on the task at hand. Passing the audition was crucial.

When I returned to Minjung, a petite young woman accompanied her. She had red-dyed hair worn half up in a high bun and a pair of circle-lensed glasses adorned her small face.

"Chloe, this is Intern Yang Bora. She'll help you practice the script," Minjung said.

"Nice to meet you, Intern Yang," I said.

"Actor Chloe, let's give it our best shot." Bora beamed.

One floor up, we stopped outside practice room D.

"Here we are," Minjung said. "All yours for the next hour. Unfortunately, I can't stay. I have work to do. I'll see you after the audition."

Bora showed me into the room. A TV screen was mounted on the wall at one end and a whiteboard at the other. A large table stood in the centre. We sat down opposite each other, scripts in front of us.

"Louise doesn't appear until page 15, so let's start from there," Bora said.

I flipped to page 15. Bora prompted me, acting as a drunk patron at the bar where Louise works.

I read my first line. "Another beer, Mr. Cha?"

Bora frowned, unimpressed.

"Did I say it wrong?" I asked.

"Well…not *wrong* exactly. I just think you need to come across a bit bubblier."

"Another beer, Mr. Cha?" I repeated, trying to sound more lively.

Bora grimaced.

I can't even say one line right…

"Do you know about the character of Louise?" Bora asked.

"Yes. A little bit."

"Well, she's an undercover reporter, right? Who do you think is her main source of information?"

"The bar patrons?"

"Exactly. And how does she get them to talk?"

"Alcohol?"

"Yes, but also her charms. She flirts with them."

"Ah, I see! You seem to know a lot about Louise…"

"I know this script back to front. I've been helping Shin Jinseung practice as well."

"Shin Jinseung?" The name sounded vaguely familiar.

"You don't know him? He's another actor from KAM who's in this drama."

"Who does he play?"

"Officer Park Minjoon. It's the lead male role."

"Oh…So if I get the part, I'll be working with him…"

"That's right." Bora sighed. "So lucky…In the third episode, there's a scene—"

Her phone beeped, diverting her attention.

"*Aigoo*! We've already wasted ten minutes. Let's get back to the script."

With Bora's advice, I nailed the bar scene and we moved on to the next scene featuring Louise.

"Oh! This scene has Officer Park in it," I said.

"Yes. There are quite a few scenes between Louise and Officer Park. They're friends. He's the only person who she shows her intelligent side. You can act more natural with him."

"Got it."

We read through the scene. Since I just had to act like myself, it came easily to me.

"That's good," Bora said. "Shall we try everything again? This time, try not to rely on the script."

I closed my script. "I'm ready."

We started over from the top. I repeated my lines over and over until they were drilled into my head. Fully focused on the script, I jumped when Bora's phone rang.

"Yes, Mr. Kim?" she answered. "…I see…Yes…Room D…"

She put down her phone. "PD Im Nara is here. It's time for your audition."

The sound of high heels clicking on the floor intensified as Im Nara approached. I gulped, feeling apprehensive.

She appeared at the door—a woman in her forties, immaculately dressed in a beige pant suit, a designer bag tucked under her arm. Her fierce eyes locked onto mine. I stood up and bowed.

"You must be Chloe Gibson. I'm Im Nara—PD of Hidden History."

She offered her hand. I shook it firmly.

"Nice to meet you, PD-nim."

Nara turned to Bora. "And who are you?"

"Intern Yang Bora. Can I get you anything to drink, PD-nim? Tea, coffee…?"

"A glass of water will be fine, thank you."

"Yes. Right away." Bora hurried off.

Nara pulled out a chair and sat down. I followed suit, lowering myself into a chair, my heart pounding.

Nara studied me. Her red lips curled into a half-smile. "Well, you certainly look the part…But can you act?"

"I'll do my best, PD-nim."

"Your best is certainly expected."

Heat rushed to my cheeks.

Bora returned with two glasses of water. She placed one in front of Nara, and one in front of me. I drank, trying to bring my soaring temperature back down.

"Could I please watch the audition?" Bora asked.

"That's fine. Take a seat," Nara said.

Bora sat at the back of the room. She gave me a thumbs-up and mouthed, "*Hwaiting!*"

Nara retrieved a leather-bound notebook from her handbag. She opened it and jotted down a few preliminary notes.

"Right. Let's begin," she said at last. "Stand up there."

"Should I leave the script?"

"Yes. I'll prompt you if you get stuck."

I took my place at the front, standing as straight as my back would allow.

"Intern, I have a job for you," Nara said.

"Yes?"

"Could you please film the audition on your phone?"

"Yes, PD-nim." Bora tapped at her phone screen then positioned the camera lens towards me.

"All set?" Nara asked. "From your first line. Go."

I took a deep breath, then with all the confidence I could muster, I delivered my lines. I even added a little bit of movement to spice things up.

While I acted, Nara sat with her arms folded and a bored expression on her face. She read back to me in flat, monotone delivery. I pushed through, not letting her behaviour detract from my performance.

"Stop," Nara said, after just a few lines. "That's enough."

Did I do something wrong?

"Stop recording. Here." Na-Jung passed Bora her business card. "Email the clip to me."

Is that it? How could she reach a decision on just that?

"I've sent it," Bora said.

"Perfect. Excuse me for a moment."

"Wait!" I said, the word surprising me as it tumbled from my lips.

Nara stopped. "Yes?"

"I have something to say."

She tapped her foot impatiently. "Go on."

"The thing is, Louise and I have something in common. She's the only foreigner in her town. I know what that's like. When I attended Tongyeong High School for a year, I was the only foreign student. I can relate to Louise in this way. Maybe it will help me portray her."

"…I see."

I couldn't tell whether my little speech had helped or hindered my chances. Nara left the room, closing the door behind her.

I looked at Bora, confused. "What's happening?"

She shrugged. "I guess we'll just have to wait and see."

"Was my acting okay?"

"I think so."

"Hmmm…"

I sank into my chair, sighing. A little voice at the back of my head told me that I'd missed my chance. Why else did Nara seem so unimpressed?

Every minute which passed felt like torture. I practically jumped out of my skin when Nara swept back in.

"A decision has been made," she said.

7

My muscles tensed. I couldn't read Nara's blank expression. Then, slowly, the corners of her mouth lifted into a smile.

"I want you to play Louise," she said.

I thought I must have misheard. "Sorry?"

"The producer agrees. He watched the clip."

"So…I passed the audition?"

"You look surprised."

"It just happened so fast…"

"Chloe, I've auditioned hundreds of people in my time. I can tell very quickly whether I want to work with someone or not."

"Congratulations!" Bora beamed. "I'm so happy for you! I'll text Seo Minjung the news."

Nara checked her watch. "I've got to run. Producer Kang will send the paperwork through to Mr. Kim. You'll need to sign it today."

"Yes, PD-nim."

"See you on set."

"See you."

She rushed away. I could hear her talking on her phone as she walked.

Bora squealed with delight and grabbed my hands. "This is so awesome! You're going to be great."

I was dumbstruck. The reality of the situation still hadn't sunk in.

"Oh! Minjung's calling." Bora answered her phone.

I'm going to be in a K-drama. My heart raced. *I'm actually going to be in a K-drama.*

Bora put her phone down. "Minjung invited us for lunch with her and Mr. Kim. We'll meet in the restaurant next door."

"Intern Yang, this is real, right? I'm not dreaming?"

"It's real. I can pinch you if you want."

I shook myself and let out a high-pitched yelp of joy. "Yes!" I yelled, punching the air.

"That's right. Let it all out." Bora watched on, amused.

After I had calmed down, I excused myself to go and make a call. I needed to tell my best friend, Han Seri, the news. She and I had known each other since we were thirteen years old. We had been host sisters twice—first, when my family hosted her on a three-month exchange, and again, when her family hosted me on my one-year exchange to Korea. Seri introduced me to K-dramas. The fact that I was going to act in one would no doubt blow her mind.

"Hello?" Seri answered.

"Seri, it's me, Chloe."

"Chloe! It's nice to hear your voice." She spoke in English. Her fluency had improved greatly since moving to Melbourne. "We haven't spoken in a wee while."

"I have big news!"

"Oooh. Well, what is it then?"

I paused for effect before letting it spill out. "I'm going to be in a K-drama!"

Seri took a moment to process what I said. "Wait, what? Slow down and explain. A K-drama?"

"A talent scout from KAM Entertainment spotted me last night and asked me to audition for a role in a new drama. I had the audition today and I passed. I'm going to be in a K-drama."

"Oh my God! This isn't a joke, is it?"

"I'm completely serious."

"What happened to teaching English?"

"Long story short, that didn't work out. But now I get to act in a K-drama instead!"

Seri let out a shriek of joy. "I can't believe it!"

"Neither can I!"

"This is like our childhood dreams come true."

"I know!"

"Which actors are in the drama?"

"I only know about one actor so far. Shin…" My mind went blank. "Shin something."

"That's helpful."

"I don't know very much, but I'll tell you everything as soon as I find out."

"This is so exciting!"

"It feels surreal."

"What's the drama called?"

"Hidden History."

"I'll look it up."

"You'll probably find out more than me. Anyway, I've got to go. Heading to a celebratory lunch."

"You lucky thing."

"Let's chat again soon."

"Definitely. Don't leave me hanging."

"Bye, Seri."

"Buh-bye."

After ending the call, I returned to Bora.

"Are you hungry?" she asked.

"Starving," I replied.

We made the short trip to the nearby barbecue restaurant. Its warm interior featured exposed brick walls and lights hanging low over wooden tables and chairs. The smell of sizzling meat permeated the air.

Minjung and Mr. Kim had already arrived. They beckoned us to their table, grins plastered on their faces.

"There's the star of the day!" Mr. Kim said. "Let's celebrate. Lunch is on me."

We ordered a vast array of delicious small dishes to share.

"I hear you passed the audition with flying colours," Mr. Kim said.

"She did!" Bora said. "I was there."

"I couldn't have done it without your help, Intern Yang," I said.

"Awww, I didn't do much."

"Both of you did a very good job," Mr. Kim said. "Intern, I'd like you to keep helping Chloe. You and Manager Bong will already be on set assisting Jinseung, so you can look after Chloe as well."

"Yes, sir."

Bora and I exchanged delighted looks.

Mr. Kim continued. "Chloe, the lawyers are putting your contract together as we speak. It should be ready for you to sign this afternoon. Shooting begins on Thursday. You'll receive a call sheet tomorrow which will tell you the location and the time you need to be there. I believe it will be mostly filmed at the production studio in Yongin."

I nodded along, although it was a lot of information to take in.

"Do you have a Korean bank account?" Mr. Kim asked.

"No, not yet."

"I'll get the lawyers to sort that out too. We can also give you a small advance. Minjung told me about your money situation."

"That would be great. Thank you. What about accommodation? I slept on Minjung's couch last night…"

"Oh! I've found an apartment which looks promising," Minjung said. "Hopefully you'll be able to move in today if all goes well."

"Thanks, Minjung! That's a relief."

My whole body relaxed, all of my doubts and concerns melting away. *Everything's working out…*

In high spirits, we tucked into the steaming dishes of *bulgogi, galbi, bibimbap*, and *samgyupsal gui*, plus heaping rice and vegetable side dishes. I hadn't eaten so well in a long time. I let out a satisfied sigh once full.

Mr. Kim's phone began to ring. He swallowed his mouthful before answering. "*Yeoboseyo?* Oh, Jinseung…you heard?…Uh huh. When?…All right…See you soon."

"Jinseung!" Bora whispered to me, sounding excited.

Mr. Kim set down his phone. "That was Actor Shin Jinseung. He heard about the casting and wants to meet you since you'll be working together."

"Shin Jinseung wants to meet *me*?" I said.

"Of course. He's at KAM. Meet him when we get back."

Shin Jinseung…Despite years of K-drama watching, I didn't

think I'd seen him in anything before. I wondered what he was like. Young? Handsome? Cute?

I didn't have to wonder for long. Back at KAM, Bora took me up to a lounge on the eighth floor where we had agreed to meet Jinseung. A man was there, back turned to us—he was tall and a bit chubby, with short black hair. *Is he Shin Jinseung?* He turned around. He was a man in his forties with a soft, kind-looking face. I peered at him, confused. He didn't look like the typical lead K-drama star.

"Manager Bong, where's actor Shin?" Bora asked.

Ahhh…he's Jinseung's manager.

"He'll be back in a minute." He turned to me. "So you're Chloe? I'm Bong Changsoo, manager of Shin Jinseung." He shook my hand.

"Nice to meet you."

Something caught his eye behind me. "Oh, he's here."

I turned around and saw him approaching. *No…It can't be…* The wavy-haired, cute guy I had encountered in the bathroom earlier that day. He stared at me, looking startled. My face grew hot with embarrassment.

8

S hin Jinseung's jaw clenched and unclenched as he studied me. He bit his lip. I shifted on my feet, nervous that he would bring up the bathroom incident.

"Shin Jinseung, this is Chloe Gibson," Changsoo said.

"Hello." I lowered my head.

Jinseung bowed back, grinning.

We sat down on the two large suede couches around a coffee table, Bora and I next to each other, Jinseung opposite us.

"Does anyone want a drink?" Changsoo asked.

"A coffee," Jinseung said.

"Me too," Bora said.

"And you, Chloe? Coffees all round?"

"Yes, please."

Changsoo got to work in the small kitchen area, pulling mismatched mugs from the cupboard.

"So, how come we weren't introduced sooner?" Jinseung asked, leaning towards me, head resting in his hands.

"She only came to KAM today," Bora explained. "Seo Minjung scouted her last night."

Jinseung raised a sceptical brow. "You were found yesterday, and you've already nabbed a drama role?"

I nodded. "It surprises me as well. I arrived in Seoul yesterday to be an English teacher. Now, 24 hours later, here I am."

"*Aigoo*. After years of formal acting training I didn't even get a role that big to start."

"You sound bitter, Actor-nim," Changsoo chided, filling the mugs with boiling water.

Jinseung laughed. "Not bitter. Just baffled."

"I'm just lucky," I said. "It's like the stars were aligned just right for this to happen."

"Must be fate," Bora said dreamily.

"Fate? Hmmm…" Jinseung had a faraway look in his eyes.

Changsoo brought a tray of coffees over and sat next to Jinseung. "Cheer up, Actor-nim. You never know, Officer Park could be your breakout role." He passed Jinseung his coffee.

"That's what I'm hoping for."

"Officer Park is Actor-nim's first lead role," Changsoo explained. "Before this he has only had second lead and supporting roles."

"But he's still really popular!" Bora said.

Changsoo sipped his coffee, then he looked up, a thought striking him. "Chloe, did you know that you're playing Officer Park's love interest in this drama?"

"What?" I spluttered, managing to spray coffee before I could cover my mouth.

"*Omo*." Bora handed me a napkin.

"Love interest might be going a bit too far," Jinseung said dismissively.

"Why? It seems like Officer Park likes Louise," Changsoo said.

"I think so too," Bora said.

I chewed my lip. *Are we really going to play love interests?* I made a mental note to ask for more episode scripts so I could see for myself.

"*Aigoo.* Look at the time. I need to take you to your hair appointment," Changsoo said to Jinseung.

"Hair appointment?" Bora said, wide-eyed.

"They want my hair short for the drama," Jinseung said as he got up, leaving behind his half-drunk coffee.

"Noooo!"

"It was nice meeting you, Chloe," Changsoo said.

I bowed.

"See you soon," Jinseung said.

"Goodbye Actor-nim, uh, *Seonbae-nim*," I said.

"His hair…his precious hair…" Bora lamented as Jinseung left the room. She withered on the couch, sulking.

I finished the rest of my coffee while I arranged my thoughts.

"So, what do you think of Shin Jinseung?" Bora asked, clearing the mugs from the coffee table.

"He's nice. He seems humble."

"Isn't he good-looking?" She sighed.

"Yeah, he's cute." I couldn't deny it.

"He's single too! Not that he's even considering dating anyone right now. Whenever he dates, his career slows down. 'The dating curse,' he calls it. Not to mention Mr. Kim would murder him if he ever caused a scandal—he's at such a crucial stage in his career."

"I've heard that most Korean celebrities won't date, at least not publicly."

"That's right. Such a shame…" She sighed again before changing the subject. "Say, why did Jinseung have that weird expression on his face when he first saw you?"

"You noticed that? It's, well…Actually, this wasn't the first time we saw each other."

"What do you mean?"

"I accidentally walked into the men's bathroom this morning…and I saw him…"

"*Omo*. Did you see his—?"

"No. I didn't see anything."

Bora pouted. "What a pity."

We looked at each other before cracking up with laughter.

9

As I signed my name across the dotted line on the final contract, a thought crossed my mind that the company was taking advantage of me. *But what else can I do?*

It had taken me hours to go through the contract. Although my Korean language skills were good, my proficiency didn't extend to legal jargon. I used an app to translate as much as I could, but I would have preferred to get everything properly translated and looked over by a lawyer. Unfortunately, time was of the essence.

"Is that everything?" Mr. Kim peered across his desk.

"I think so," I replied.

"Excellent." He combed through the stack of documents, checking I had signed all the necessary pages. When satisfied, he straightened the pile and placed it neatly to the side. He stood up. "Congratulations, Actor Chloe. You're now signed to KAM." He shook my hand. "Your contract will last through the filming of Hidden History. Unfortunately, at this stage we can't promise an extension. Roles such as this are a rarity."

"I understand. Thank you, Mr. Kim."

"It's been a whirlwind day, hasn't it? You should go home and get some rest. You're probably still jet-lagged, right?"

"Home…"

"Ah. Talk to Minjung. She should have something arranged for you."

"Yes, Mr. Kim."

He showed me to the door. "You'll do well, Actor Chloe."

"Thank you, Mr. Kim."

"Do you remember the way to Minjung's desk?"

"Yes."

"Okay. See you around. Call me if you need anything."

I bowed to him before leaving to find Minjung. *Now, which way was it?* I looked from left to right, trying to recall the direction. I scratched my head. *Hmmmm…*Following my gut, I walked the corridors until I made it to the open-plan office where Minjung worked. I crossed the floor to her desk.

"Minjung-ssi…" I said.

She looked up. "Oh! Actor-nim. I have something for you." She searched her messy desk. "Where did I put it? Aha!" She held up a card hanging from a blue lanyard. "Here's your ID card. Now you can come and go from the building as you please."

"Thanks!" I took the card and stuffed it in my pocket. "Mr. Kim said I can go now. I was wondering if…"

"Don't worry. You won't need to sleep on my couch again. I managed to find you a place. It's a serviced studio apartment in Seocho-dong. The rent will be deducted from your pay. I hope it will suit your needs."

"I'll just be happy to have a roof over my head."

"I'll text Intern Yang. She can drive you there. I've already had her collect your luggage from my place."

She sent the message and a moment later Bora texted back.

"She'll meet you at the carpark. Let's go."

Minjung took me down to the underground carpark. Bora waved from a black SUV.

Before leaving, I said goodbye to Minjung. "Thank you for everything. I don't know how things would have ended up if I hadn't met you."

Minjung smiled. "It's thanks to you that the production of Hidden History can start without a hitch. I look forward to watching you."

"Hopefully I'll see you again before filming starts."

"Let's keep in touch anyway."

"That would be great."

"Take care. Hope everything's okay with the apartment. Call me if there's anything you need."

"I will. Thank you."

We bowed to each other then parted ways.

Bora stood impatiently outside the car. I rushed over to her. She opened the door to the back seat and ushered me in.

"Can't I sit in the front?" I asked.

"Oh? Okay."

We hopped into the car next to each other. Before I even put my seatbelt on, Bora zoomed away to the exit. She drove erratically through the darkening streets of Seoul. A sudden turn off made me lurch in my seat. "Gyaaa!"

"Oh. Sorry. I'm not a very good driver."

"I can tell."

"When I got this job, I realised that I needed a driver's licence, so I had to quickly learn and pass the test."

"How did you pass?"

"I don't know."

I clutched the edges of my seat for dear life as Bora drove.

I didn't catch my breath until we finally turned down the driveway to an apartment building and parked.

"This is it," Bora said. "Sapphire Apartments."

The high-rise building had a facade of shiny, blue-tinted glass. Several small shops occupied the ground level, including a convenience store, café, and a pharmacy.

"Your apartment is on the seventeenth floor. I'll go up with you," Bora said. She got out and grabbed my luggage from the boot.

"I'll take that," I said, reaching for my suitcase.

"Let me do it," Bora insisted. Despite her small size, she didn't seem to struggle with my heavy bags.

We proceeded to the lobby, classy and clean, with a small seating area, mailboxes, and a reception desk. Bora retrieved my access card from reception.

It was smooth sailing to the seventeenth floor.

"Here we are. Key code is 9409. Make sure to change it later." Bora typed in the code then pushed open the door.

The apartment was compact but perfectly adequate. Storage cupboards on the left, bathroom on the right. Farther down, a kitchen, and at the far end, a double bed by the window. The appliances and furniture looked modern and in good condition. The room was quiet, and the air felt warm and dry. I immediately felt at ease.

"It's probably smaller than you're used to, right?" Bora asked.

"No. It's cozy. I like it."

Truthfully, I was just glad to have a place to stay. It seemed comfortable and secure, and that's all that mattered after everything I had been through. I would be happy to call this apartment my home—at least until the end of my acting gig. I wouldn't be able to afford the rent after that.

"The location can't be beaten." Bora gazed out the window at the vast metropolis of buildings, their windows lighting up as night fell.

"Whereabouts do you live?" I asked.

"Gwacheon. I still live with my parents. They won't let me move out. Not that I could afford to, anyway."

"This is my first time living alone. I've only lived with my parents or with flatmates before."

"You're lucky. So much freedom!"

"Yeah. I guess I never really thought about it."

Bora sighed. "Oh well. I'll leave you to it. You must be looking forward to unpacking and getting settled."

"I would ask you to stay and have a drink, but I don't have anything to give you."

"That's all right. Next time!"

"Okay. Next time."

"See you soon!"

"Bora-ssi—"

"What?"

"Drive safe."

She stuck her tongue out at me as she closed the door.

Alone in the apartment, the first thing I did was collapse on the bed. Since the moment I had arrived in Seoul, it felt like I was on a rollercoaster. In just two days, more had happened to me than in my entire life. My body ached. My head reeled.

I lay like that for a while until I found the resolve to put away my stuff. Clothes into the drawers, books onto shelves, and everything else into cupboards.

With everything stored in its rightful place, I turned to another piece of life admin. I messaged my host parents in Tongyeong, letting them know I had arrived in Korea. I had already let my parents know I had arrived but left out all the nitty gritty details. I'd deal with that another day.

By the time that was done, my stomach growled. I popped down to the convenience store and bought instant *ramyeon* to eat for dinner. I slurped the hot, spicy noodles while reading articles and watching videos about Hidden History. To my delight, I learned that Baek Yena played the other lead character in the series. She was an actor I had admired for a long time. I couldn't wait to meet her.

Shin Jinseung also featured prominently in the Hidden History press coverage. I found myself browsing for information about him, and soon enough I fell down a rabbit hole of interviews and photoshoots.

I was midway through typing *Shin Jinseung shirtless* into the search bar when my phone rang, and I hurriedly closed the tab, feeling guilty.

"*Yeoboseyo?*" I answered.

"Actor-nim, this is Bong Changsoo. Shin Jinseung would like to rehearse with you tomorrow. Is that okay with you?"

"Yes. Of course," I stuttered.

"Great. I'll let him know. I'll book in a practice room. See you tomorrow."

10

I sat alone in the practice room, fully absorbed in reading my script, when a deep male voice startled me.

"That's cute."

I looked up and saw Jinseung. His new short hairstyle lent him a more mature look. He wore jeans, a hoodie, and a pair of glasses with black wire frames. I recalled the pictures I had viewed of him last night and how handsome he looked, but he looked even better in real life.

"What's cute?" I asked, raising an eyebrow.

"You bite your lip when you're concentrating," he explained.

"I do?"

"You were just doing it."

"Oh, was I?"

"Have you eaten breakfast?"

"No."

He dropped a plastic bag on the table. "Eat."

"What's this?" I opened the bag and found a sandwich and a bottle of orange juice. "Can I have this?"

"Yes. I ate mine on the way here."

He took a seat next to me on the couch.

I nibbled on the sandwich self-consciously.

"Do you recognise me?" he asked, suddenly.

I felt my face turn red. *Is he really bringing this up now?*

"I walked in on you before," I mumbled.

Jinseung laughed. "I'm not referring to that."

"Oh."

"I mean, we know each other."

I stopped eating. "What? How could that be possible? We just met."

"Tong…yeong…" he said slowly.

No…Could it be?

"Tongyeong? You know me from Tongyeong?"

"You lived in Tongyeong for a while. Am I right?"

"Yes. How do you know that?"

"We went to the same high school. You probably don't remember me. I was your *seonbae*. We didn't interact much since we weren't in the same year group, but you stuck out as the only foreigner."

I went to high school with Shin Jinseung and I didn't even know it.

"*Aigoo*. What a coincidence," I uttered.

"It must be fate," Jinseung mused.

"Huh?"

"Intern said that, remember?"

"That's right! Little did she know."

"I got a shock when I saw you in the bathroom. Obviously, I didn't expect to see a girl there, but I also felt a stab of recognition. When I heard your name, it confirmed it."

"I can't believe it."

"It's insane, right?"

"Sorry I didn't recognise you."

"That's okay. My image has changed a lot since I started acting."

I chewed over this interesting development while finishing the sandwich. *So Jinseung knew me all along…What a strange turn of events.* Somehow it made me feel more comfortable about working with him. We had common ground.

"Shall we practice our first scene together?" Jinseung asked once I had finished eating.

"Okay. Let's do it."

"It's late at night in the town." Jinseung paced the room as he set the scene. "You've just finished up at the bar, and you're walking home. I'm out on patrol, when I notice you and pull over."

"The couch can be your car?"

"Good idea."

Jinseung sat down and grasped an invisible steering wheel. He pretended to pull over and wind down the window.

"Louise," he said, in character.

I stopped and turned to him. "Officer Park."

"It's late. What are you doing walking around by yourself?"

"I just finished my shift. I'm heading home."

"You're not driving?"

"My car's out of action. It's being repaired."

"Then let me give you a ride home."

"Really? Is that okay?"

"Of course. It's my job to make sure everyone stays safe in this neighbourhood. Hop in."

I mimed opening the passenger door, then sat down beside him.

"Are you okay?" Jinseung asked.

"It's been a long night."

At that point, there was a knock on the practice room door. It pulled us both out of the scene. Jinseung sighed. "Come in!" he barked.

It was Bora, holding two takeaway coffee cups. "Did I interrupt? Oh, sorry." She placed the coffee cups on the table. "Drink this and keep your energy levels up."

"Thanks," I said.

"Do you need any help with practicing?"

"I would have asked you to stay and prompt, but it doesn't seem like we need it," Jinseung said. He turned to me. "You know your lines perfectly already."

I shrugged. "I'm good at memorising."

"Well, just text me if you need me and I'll come right over," Bora said. She closed the door behind her.

"Now, where were we?" Jinseung said, flipping through his script.

After finding our place, we got back into character and continued rehearsing the scene, free from interruption.

When we finished, I looked to Jinseung, bracing myself for criticism. Instead, I was met by an intrigued smile.

"I have to admit, I was worried to hear PD-nim had cast someone with no drama experience. But it turns out I had nothing to worry about. You're a natural."

I exhaled, relieved. *So at least my acting is okay…*

Jinseung continued. "There's room for improvement, of course, but I think you can do a good job."

"Thank you, *seonbae-nim*. That's encouraging."

We ran through the scene a couple more times and Jinseung gave me some helpful pointers.

"Time to move on to episode two?" he suggested, satisfied with our progress.

"I only have the first episode script…"

"Here. Use mine for now. I can get by without it."

We rehearsed our scenes together in the second episode. I relied on the script while Jinseung read from memory.

Once we had exhausted those scenes, we decided to work separately for the rest of the day—Jinseung had many more scenes to learn that I wasn't involved in. I had offered to help, but he declined.

"I'll ask Intern or Changsoo *Hyung* to run through them with me," he explained. "It's better for you to focus on your own lines."

"Okay."

"You should get the scripts for episode two and three. That's all that's been released so far. Ask Changsoo. He'll be able to sort that out for you."

"All right. Thank you."

I was about to leave when Jinseung spoke up again.

"Chloe…do you know what happens in episode three?" he asked, a nervous edge to his voice.

"Louise dies, right?"

"Yes. But there's, uh, something else…"

"What is it?"

"You should read the script."

"Why? What happens in episode three?"

"You'll see."

———

Curious about what Jinseung was referring to, I called Changsoo to ask him to prepare the scripts for me.

"No problem, Actor-nim. I'll get them sorted," he said.

After eating lunch, I returned to KAM and met Changsoo on the third floor. He worked in a small office along with other staff in Jinseung's team. His clean and organised desk featured a framed photograph of him posing and making heart signs with Jinseung. *How sweet! Changsoo must care a lot for Jinseung.*

"Here you go," he passed me the scripts. "These were actually delivered yesterday, but reception didn't know who they were for."

"That's understandable. I'm new."

"In future, anything addressed to you will come to my office and I'll let you know."

"Thank you, Manager Bong."

"I've booked you practice room D for the rest of the afternoon. Off you go. Learn those lines." He shooed me away, grinning warmly.

"Manager Bong…"

"Yes?"

"What happens in episode three? *Seonbae-nim* said something about it…"

Changsoo scratched his head. "Episode three…Oh, that!"

"What is it?"

He chuckled. "You've got the script now. Read it and find out."

"So, you won't tell me either? Hmmm…what could it be?"

I made my way to the practice room, still pondering over the third episode.

Afternoon sunlight poured in the practice room window. It warmed my back when I sat down at the table. Not wanting to jump ahead and spoil things, I started reading from episode two, before moving on to the third episode.

By the time I had reached the halfway point of episode

three, I still hadn't discovered what it was that Jinseung had warned me about. Then, finally, I saw what he meant. A kiss scene. A kiss scene between Louise and Officer Park.

11

───────

No…I must be seeing things. I reread the passage to make sure my mind wasn't playing tricks on me, but it was there in clear print—*Louise kisses Officer Park. I have to kiss Jinseung.* Now his shy reaction made sense. *A kiss scene…I have to do a kiss scene…and with Jinseung!*

I couldn't concentrate. As I tried to learn my lines, my mind kept travelling back to the kiss scene…the thought of Jinseung's lips on mine…*It won't be too embarrassing, will it?* I recalled the usual K-drama kiss scenes. That weird, frozen, close-mouthed lip press. Completely passionless. *That's what it will be like. I wonder whether Jinseung has a lot of experience with kiss scenes…*

I remained curious for the rest of the day, and as soon as I got home, I grabbed my laptop and searched *Shin Jinseung kiss scene*. A few results popped up. *Let's see…*

I watched the first video intently. Jinseung and his co-star, Choi Miyoung, are walking along together when a downpour suddenly starts. They run for cover under the eaves of a temple. Soaking wet and panting, they look at each other, expressions turning serious. They start to kiss. A realistic, passionate kiss.

*Oh my…*I fanned myself, suddenly feeling hot.

I scrolled through the comments beneath the video.

"So romantic."

"He is a good kisser!"

"I love his kiss scenes."

I worked my way through the other video clips and none of his kisses were the stiff, close-lipped kind. *So, looks like Jinseung doesn't hold back…*

I stroked my lips unconsciously as I pictured how our kiss might unfold. *My character is assertive, so I must go for it without hesitation, in one swift movement. Our lips touch…*

A notification popped up on my screen, interrupting my train of thought. *Hidden History day 1 call sheet.* I opened the email, ready to see what the first day's shoot had in store for me. My call time struck me first. I needed to be at the production studio by 5:30am for costume, hair, and makeup. I groaned internally, before resolving to get myself tucked up in bed nice and early.

———

A loud noise pierced my dream and yanked me into consciousness. *Is it time to get up already?* Forcing my eyes to stay open, I groped in the darkness for my phone and turned off the alarm. 4:30am. *Ugh.* I heaved myself out of bed and hurried to get ready. While in the process of putting my clothes on, I received a text message:

Bora: We're nearly at your apartment.

Gah! I quickly piled on the rest of my clothes and grabbed the bag I had pre-packed the night before.

Still half-asleep, I took the elevator down and waited outside the building, huddled in a padded down jacket, beanie, and scarf. My breath came out in puffs of mist in the pitch-black air.

A couple minutes later, a black van rolled up. Changsoo occupied the driver's seat while Bora sat in the passenger seat. Bora hopped out and opened the door for me. Jinseung sat in the back. He appeared calm and collected, studying his script while sipping from an extra-large cup of coffee. I slid in next to him and pulled on my seat belt, feeling shyer than usual in his presence.

"How are you feeling, Actor Chloe?" Changsoo asked as he drove. "Ready to take on the day?"

"Absolutely," I said, then failed to stifle a humongous yawn.

Jinseung put his script down. "Let me guess. You're not a morning person?"

"Correct," I admitted.

"You better get used to early mornings. And late nights."

"*Aigoo.*"

"He's winding you up," Changsoo said. "It won't be too bad for you since you're not in that many scenes. Actor Shin has it much worse."

"Here." Jinseung pulled another coffee from the cupholder and passed it to me. "There's an extra shot in there. It might help you wake up."

"Thanks." I accepted it eagerly.

The strong coffee warmed me to the core.

"Your call time is probably so early because you haven't

been fitted for wardrobe yet," Changsoo explained. "They'll need to sort all that out before they can film your scenes."

"Ah. I see."

"It's going to be a long day." Sighing, Jinseung returned his attention to his script.

I watched him as I drank my coffee. He had a focused expression on his face, a small crease between his brows. I found my gaze wandering down to his lips, reminding me that I would soon have to kiss him. "*Seonbae-nim…*"

"Yes?"

"I read the third episode script."

He sniggered. "You did? Is that why you've been staring at my mouth?"

Damn. He noticed that? "I have not!" I retorted.

"You're so lucky," Bora piped up. "Lots of girls would kill to be in your position."

"That's right," Jinseung teased.

"I'm actually pretty nervous about the whole thing," I confessed.

"Don't worry. I've done it a few times before. You're in safe hands. I'll guide you."

"Such a gentleman!" Bora said.

Jinseung wiggled his eyebrows seductively at me, making me laugh.

"It's nice to see you two getting along so well," Changsoo remarked. "It will help your on-screen chemistry."

"Want to know something funny?" Jinseung asked.

"What is it?"

"Chloe and I went to high school together."

"How can that be? Are you joking?"

"It's true," I said. "I did a high school exchange to Tongyeong for one year."

"*Aigoo.* What are the chances?"

"What was Chloe like in high school?" Bora asked.

"All the boys liked her," Jinseung said.

"Really? So she was popular…"

"Only because I was the only foreigner in the school!" I retorted. "They probably thought I was exotic or something."

"What about you, Actor Shin? Did *you* like her?" Bora asked.

"Don't be ridiculous," he spluttered.

It was a thirty-minute drive to the production studio in Yongin. We passed through a gated area to reach a huge, windowless building which looked like a warehouse. Changsoo parked outside.

The four of us approached the building. Two production assistants flanked the main entrance, taking down the names of people arriving in a register. Changsoo announced our arrival.

"You're both due in wardrobe," the man with the register said. "Make your way to the dressing rooms." He pointed us to an external staircase at the side of the building.

We climbed the staircase and entered a door which led to a blue-carpeted corridor with small rooms off each side.

I noticed one of the rooms had Jinseung's name on the door.

"Oh! This is your dressing room," I said.

Jinseung pushed open the door and inspected the room. It contained a couch, dressing table, and clothes rack full of outfits.

"I guess I'll get settled in," he said. "See you on set later."

Changsoo joined him.

Bora stayed with me and we searched the corridor for my dressing room. Halfway down, we bumped into an *ajumma*

with wild, curly hair, her neck and wrists piled with an abundance of jewellery.

"Are you Chloe Gibson?" she asked.

"Yes."

"Through here, my dear. I'll get you fitted."

She ushered us into a large room filled with racks of clothes
and tables brimming with accessories. Then my eyes fell upon
the other woman in the room. My heart skipped a beat.

Bora gasped. "*Omo*. It's Baek Yena!"

12

Baek Yena looked just as cool and attractive in real life as she did in the dramas and movies I'd seen her in. She wore black from head to toe. Her blunt bob haircut and choppy fringe framed a round face with almond eyes and doll-like lips. She stood with her arms folded, an intrigued expression on her face.

"Hello," she said, eyebrow raised.

"Actor Baek Yena, I'm a big fan," Bora gushed.

"Oh? Thank you. Are you two actors?"

Bora giggled. "Do I look like I could be an actor?"

"I'm one of the actors," I said. "My name is Chloe Gibson. I'm playing Louise."

Yena's expression brightened. "So you're the replacement for Tamara? You're pretty! And you speak Korean so well!"

"Thank you."

She motioned to Bora who continued giggling away. "Is she your manager?"

"She's an intern from KAM Entertainment. Her name is Yang Bora."

"Ahhh…KAM. So you know Shin Jinseung then?"

"That's right."

Yena smiled. "I can picture it…"

"Sorry?"

"You and Shin Jinseung. I think you'll look good together on-screen."

"Really?"

"Yes. I can see why PD-nim cast you."

"You're too kind." I blushed profusely. "I can't wait to work with you. I love your dramas."

"I'm sure we'll have a few scenes together. It's gonna be great!"

The wardrobe *ajumma* approached Yena with a measuring tape and started wrapping it around her body and jotting numbers down on a notepad.

"My schedule's been so hectic," Yena said with a sigh. "I haven't had a chance to get fitted until now."

Once Yena's measurements had been taken, the *ajumma* turned the measuring tape on me.

"Take off your jacket," she said.

I shrugged it off and tried not to squirm too much as she coiled the tape around different parts of my body.

At last, she withdrew the tape and I relaxed.

"All done," she said. "Both of you, please try to maintain your weight—it will make my job a lot easier."

"*Aigoo*…You're asking the impossible there," Yena said under her breath.

"What was that?"

"Nothing!"

———

After trying on an abundance of outfits, we were sent to hair and makeup. I emerged several hours later, completely transformed. Standing before the full-length mirror in my dressing room, I examined myself from every angle. The slinky black blouse, unbuttoned down to the middle of my chest, revealed a not-so-subtle glimpse of cleavage. It was tucked into a denim miniskirt—perhaps the shortest skirt I'd ever worn in my life. A pair of stiletto heels further elongated my bare legs, and a gold choker with a crystal pendant adorned my neck. I wore my hair out. Previously dry and tangled, it had been trimmed and tamed into glossy, loose curls. Makeup consisted of a pale wash of shimmery eyeshadow above kitten eyes, with soft, peachy lips and cheeks on a canvas of flawless glass skin.

"*Aigoo*," Bora said, watching from behind me. "You look incredible! Like, devastatingly, heartachingly beautiful."

I assessed my reflection self-consciously. I had never worn anything like this before and couldn't help but feel uncomfortable. To my eye, it seemed a little too much—even in the context of my character.

"You have a way with words, but don't you think you're over-embellishing?"

"I think she's spot on," Changsoo said, appearing behind my shoulder. "I admit I don't know much about these things, but you really do look beautiful."

I felt reassured by his kind and genuine words.

"Awww. Thank you, Manager-nim."

"How's Jinseung doing? Everything okay out there?" Bora asked.

"It's slow progress, but he's doing well. You two should come out and watch," Changsoo suggested.

"Really? Is that okay?"

"Of course. Just be sure to stay out of the way of the crew."

"You coming too, Actor-nim?"

My desire to see Jinseung and Baek Yena in action vastly overpowered my urge to stay back and study my lines.

"Yes. Let's go," I said.

Before leaving, Bora grabbed my jacket and held it out to me.

"Here. Put this back on, you must be cold."

"You're right. I'm freezing."

I pulled it on, relieved by its warmth. I also changed my shoes, unable to walk properly in heels.

Changsoo led the way down the corridor to a doorway guarded by a production assistant wearing a headset.

"Can we go through?" Changsoo asked.

"Yes. They're currently not recording. Just be quiet and stay out of the way," the assistant said. He opened the door for us.

We stepped into a huge open space with unpainted walls and a concrete floor. Moveable lights hung from metal rods running across the high ceiling. We walked carefully, dodging tripods and cords strewn haphazardly over the floor.

I gazed in awe as we passed rows of interior location sets boxed inside wooden board walls. They looked just like real rooms, furnished with impeccable detail.

Most of the crew were concentrated around one set. *That must be where they're filming*. We quietly approached.

The police station office set featured cream walls and a wood vinyl floor. Fluorescent ceiling lights shone above wooden desks topped with phones and computers. Filing cabinets and shelving units bordered the room.

Yena sat down on an orange office chair. Jinseung stood, leaning over the desk towards her. He wore a police uniform. A couple of extras sat at other desks.

A crew member stood with a clapperboard in front of the camera.

"Action," Im Nara said from the director's chair, a large monitor in front of her.

Yena and Jinseung sprang to life.

"What do you want? Can't you see I'm busy?" Yena said, eyes glued to the computer screen in front of her.

"I have a question," Jinseung said.

Yena looked up. "All right. What is it?"

"I was—"

He stopped abruptly. His eyes had wandered from Yena. He looked out past the crew, a dazed expression on his face and his mouth slightly agape.

He's looking at me, I realised. I locked eyes with him, and he snapped out of it.

"Cut!" Nara said. "Shin Jinseung, is everything okay?"

Jinseung rubbed his head sheepishly. "Sorry. I got distracted."

"Perhaps it's time we take a break…"

"Break time!" her assistant announced.

On that note, everyone promptly dispersed.

"What was that all about?" Bora asked.

"He's probably just tired. They've done so many takes," Changsoo said. "I'll go talk to him."

He hurried to Jinseung's side.

"*Aigoo*. Acting looks tough," Bora said. "But I'm sure you'll be fine!" she added, quickly.

I took a deep breath. Nerves began to set in as I contemplated the fact that it was my turn next.

"Let's get something to eat. I'm starving," Bora said.

I hesitated. "You can go on ahead. I'm going to go and read my script again. I'll be in my dressing room."

"Well, okay then. But make sure you have something to eat later."

"I will."

Bora joined the flow of cast and crew heading to the break room. I turned the opposite way, returning to my dressing room.

Alone in the small room, I studied my script, painstakingly reading, re-reading, and reciting my lines, drilling them into my brain. *I have to get this right. I can't embarrass myself.*

Deeply absorbed, I didn't even notice Jinseung enter the room until he loudly cleared his throat. He watched me, half smiling, with a knowing look in his eyes.

"Oh! *Seonbae-nim*," I said.

"Uh, sorry to interrupt. Intern told me I'd find you here. You haven't eaten yet, have you? I brought you some food."

He placed a wrapped Subway sandwich and a bottle of water down on the table.

"Thanks," I said.

"Can I sit down?"

"Go ahead."

He lowered himself onto the couch, then returned to staring at me in a way that made my skin prickle.

"You look…good." His eyes drifted down to my chest, but he swiftly averted them.

I wrapped my jacket tighter around me, self-conscious.

"Isn't it too much?" I asked.

"No."

I wondered if it had been my outfit that distracted him earlier. *Surely not…*

"I'm sorry if we broke your concentration before," I said.

"What?"

"When Intern Yang and I came to watch your scene."

Jinseung shook his head. "That was my fault. I shouldn't let myself get distracted so easily. I should be more professional as an actor."

"Well, apart from that, you looked amazing out there with Baek Yena."

"She's far more experienced than me, so I'm hoping to learn a lot from her."

"I'm looking forward to working with her too."

"How are your lines coming along?"

"Right now, I know them off by heart. But I'm scared that I'll forget them all as soon as the camera starts rolling."

"It's only natural to feel that way." He placed his hand on my shoulder. It felt strong, warm, reassuring.

"Just stay calm," he continued, "breathe, and forget everything else but the scene. Can you do that?"

"Yes, I think so. Good advice."

He lifted his hand away as if suddenly remembering himself. "I should get back on set. They'll start shooting again soon."

"Okay."

"Don't forget to eat."

I picked up the sandwich to appease him.

"See you later," he said, smiling broadly. He closed the door behind him.

I tried to resume where I had left off but found I couldn't concentrate. I touched my shoulder where Jinseung had grasped it and let out a small sigh. His cute grin flooded my thoughts…his lips which I would soon get to kiss…

I shook my head. *Be professional. Now's not the time to get feelings for my co-star.* I turned to my script again, but it seemed pointless. *Forget it.* I put the script aside. I had learned my lines as well as I possibly could. Reading them over again wouldn't help.

I ate lunch then went back to the set. Bora waved to me, beckoning me over.

"Have you got everything memorised now?" she asked.

"Yes."

"That's good." She retrieved a folding chair for me and set it down. "Sit," she urged.

I settled on the chair and watched the scene being filmed. Jinseung and Yena performed flawlessly this time, delivering their lines with full confidence. The subtle detail in their movements and facial expressions added a sense of realism. I studied them, entranced.

"Cut," Nara said, after a lengthy pause at the end of the scene.

The camera moved to shoot it all again from another angle.

As the minutes passed, I grew more and more uneasy. In the back of my mind, I worried whether I'd be able to act even half as well as them. *I'm not even a real actor*, I reminded myself. *I'm an imposter.*

During another change in camera angle, a production assistant approached me.

"Chloe Gibson?" she asked.

"Yes?"

"We're just about to wrap up this scene. You'll be up next. Please get prepared to go on shortly."

I gulped, my throat dry. *This is it.* I wobbled as I stood up. My stomach twisted into knots of apprehension. All the self-doubt which had been nibbling away at me now screamed loudly in my head.

What if I'm terrible?
What if I stuff up?
What's my first line, again?
I can't do this…
But I had no choice. I couldn't back out now.

13

I shifted nervously on my feet, trembling as I stood in position behind the bar, waiting for the shoot to begin. A buzzing sound had started in my ears, drowning out the background noise of everything around me. The clapperboard came down.

"Action," Im Nara said.

What am I meant to do? I froze, mind completely blank. Everyone stared at me expectantly.

"Cut!"

"I'm sorry…"

"Let's try that again, shall we?"

The set was dimly lit. Black stools perched under the wooden bar. Shelves stocked with liquor bottles lined the wall behind me, and fridges on the floor below glowed with a blue backlight.

Two male actors sat at the bar—Cho Dongjoo and Kim Jaehyun, playing Mr. Cha and Mr. Lee, two middle-aged men living in the fictional neighbourhood. Extras filled the tables and chairs to create a lively atmosphere.

"Relax," Cho Dongjoo said. "You'll do fine." He smiled reassuringly.

Both he and Kim Jaehyun appeared completely at ease. They had years of experience in dramas.

"Are you ready?" Nara asked.

I nodded.

Deep breaths…

"Action."

I half-choked out my line. "Another beer, Mr. Cha?"

"You read my mind," Dongjoo said, grinning. He swayed slightly, feigning drunkenness.

I took a beer from the fridge, popped open the cap, poured it into a glass, and served it to him.

"Thanks, sweetheart."

I hesitated for too long before saying my next line. Someone prompted me, and I continued.

The scene carried on in a stop-and-start fashion, usually with me forgetting an action or a line. Take after take after take ensued.

I recalled Jinseung's advice: *Just stay calm, breathe, and forget everything else but the scene*.

Stay calm…

Breathe…

Focus on the scene…

I concentrated solely on my immediate surroundings, mentally blocking out the crew and the filming equipment.

"Action."

Everything around me dissolved apart from the characters in the bar.

At last, I managed to perform an error-free take.

"Cut."

The crew started setting up for a change in camera angle,

affording me the chance to have a short break. I sat down on the fold-out chair. Bora handed me a water bottle. She massaged my shoulders. "You're doing great," she assured me.

A stylist hovered in my vicinity holding a comb and a cushion foundation compact.

"Where's Actor Shin?" I asked Bora, as the stylist patted foundation on my face and poked at my hair with the end of the comb.

"He couldn't stay and watch. He went to record some voiceover. Manager Bong is with him."

"I see." *At least Jinseung won't see me embarrass myself.*

The break was short-lived. I returned to my mark on set, prepared for the next take.

"Action."

We performed the scene over and over again. My legs ached. My head pounded. I could say my lines automatically, but my energy waned with each take, and I feared that my acting was becoming more and more lacklustre. Nara asked me many times to be bubblier, but each time it became more difficult to muster a bubbly persona. Even when I thought we achieved a good run through, Nara made us retake.

The shoot continued for hours, each take more demoralising than the last.

When we finally wrapped up the scene, I felt completely and utterly exhausted. Unable to repress how upset I felt, I fled to my dressing room, closed the door, and cried my eyes out.

Who am I fooling? I'm not cut out to be an actor. I should have just flown back home when I had the chance. These thoughts swirled in my head, mocking me.

A knock at the door made me jump. *I can't let anyone see me like this.* I tried to brush my tears away in time, but the door began to creak open.

14

I desperately wiped at my eyes as the door inched open. Through my tear-blurred vision, I saw Bora step inside. Her mouth dropped when she locked eyes on me.

"*Unnie*, are you all right?" she asked.

"No," I sniffed.

"Oh dear." She sat down by my side and wrapped an arm around my shoulders.

"I messed up the scene and made everyone suffer through all those takes." Fresh tears rolled down my cheeks.

"You didn't mess up the scene! It's normal to do that many takes."

I lifted my chin, bottom lip quivering. "Really?"

"Of course. I think most people are surprised it didn't take longer. It was a hard scene for you."

"I made so many mistakes."

"Not from where I was watching. Besides, no one expected you to be perfect. Everyone already thinks you're a hero for stepping up and filling the role at such late notice. You were fine."

"Do you really think so?"

"Yes."

Her reassuring words calmed me down. Perhaps it really didn't go as badly as I felt it did. Maybe it was all in my head…

She rummaged in her purse and extracted a packet of tissues.

"Thanks," I said, accepting them.

"I've confirmed that you're not needed for anything else today. Actor Shin is just about ready to finish up too."

I dabbed at my eyes.

"*Aigoo*. You're too hard on yourself." Bora patted my back.

"I don't know what came over me."

"You're probably overwhelmed. It's understandable. Let's go to the bathroom and wash your face. There are streaks of makeup down your cheeks."

Bora accompanied me to the bathroom. She held my hair back as I splashed warm water on my face.

"I always carry a few supplies," she explained, fishing a pouch filled with mini-sized skincare products out of her bag.

She washed my face for me, making sure to remove every scrap of makeup. Her small, soft hands soothed and relaxed me.

"There. Looking much better. You have such beautiful skin." She beamed at me.

"Thank you. I don't know what I would do without you."

"It's so stressful being an actor. You need someone to rely on."

"You're like an angel."

Bora framed her face with her hands in a display of *aegyo*, which made me giggle.

Her phone started to ring.

"It's Manager Bong." She picked up. "*Yeoboseyo?*…We're in the bathroom…Okay…See you in a few minutes."

"Was he looking for us?"

"Yes. He's with Actor Shin. They're ready to leave. Are you okay now? Shall we meet them?"

"Yes, I think so. Let's go."

After a quick stopover at my dressing room to change out of my costume, we met Jinseung and Changsoo in the van. I slumped into the seat next to Jinseung. He turned to me and ran his eyes over my face, biting his lip. I looked away, scared that it was still obvious that I had been crying.

"*Aigoo*. What a day," Changsoo said, starting the van. "And that's just the beginning. Four months of this to come."

"I think it's exciting," Bora said. "Beats sitting in an office all day."

"Is waiting on set all day so different?"

"Yes, I think so. The atmosphere is energising. By the way, Chloe did an amazing job today for a first-time actor."

Changsoo smiled. "So I heard. Well done!"

"Thanks, guys, but I realised that I have a lot to learn," I admitted.

"It must have been tough," Jinseung mused. "That was a demanding scene for a first-time actor."

"Yes, it was. But I survived." I forced a smile.

"You did. Hey, what do you like to eat?"

"Huh? Ummm…steak is my favourite."

"So, you like steak? Intern, find the best steak restaurant in the area. We're going out for dinner, my treat."

"Yuss!" Bora pumped her fist.

"That's very generous of you," Changsoo said.

"Thank you, *seonbae-nim*," I said. "Sorry for choosing steak. It's too expensive."

Jinseung grinned. "What are you saying? You should take advantage. Order the most expensive thing you want."

"Well, if you say so."

Bora searched her phone for nearby restaurants. "Oh! This one looks good. Jin Steakhouse. It's not too far away, and it's got great reviews."

"Jin Steakhouse it is," Jinseung said.

Bora typed the address into the car's GPS, and Changsoo followed the directions.

Ten minutes later, we arrived at a small strip of restaurants on a quiet suburban street. Warm light glowed from the steakhouse's windows upon its red-brick facade. Jinseung led the way through the door into the restaurant's cozy, rustic-styled interior. A gas fireplace blazed in the corner. After battling the cold all day, I felt warmed to the core.

A waiter showed us to a table with four comfy chairs. I sat next to Jinseung and opposite Bora.

"Shall we get some soju?" Jinseung asked.

"Go for it," Changsoo said.

"Do you drink, Chloe?"

"Yes. But I won't have much. I'm a lightweight."

"Is that so? Well, I'll get two bottles. That will be more than enough. I can't have a hangover tomorrow."

He ordered the soju and started pouring it into shot glasses.

"Hold on. One of us needs to drive," I said.

"I don't mind. I'll keep driving. It's my job, after all," Changsoo said.

"Wait. I've got an idea," Jinseung said. "Let's play paper scissors rock for it. The loser has to be the sober driver. Okay? Can you drive, Chloe?"

"Yes. But I'm not used to the roads here...driving on the right-hand side and all that."

"Ah. I forget that it's different in the UK. You don't have to participate then."

"No. I'll play. I'll just have to not lose."

Jinseung laughed. "Okay, good plan. Is everyone in then?"

"I'm in!" Bora said.

"Me too," Changsoo agreed.

"Round one will be Intern versus Chloe and *Hyung* versus myself. The winners will then face each other. Best two out of three," Jinseung explained.

I faced Bora. "Are you ready?"

"I was born ready," she replied.

"Paper...scissors...rock!" we cried in unison.

I chose scissors and she chose paper. I won the next round as well, with a rock versus her scissors.

"Too easy," I said.

Meanwhile, Jinseung and Changsoo were still going since they kept tying. Eventually, Jinseung won.

"Final round," Jinseung announced.

Changsoo fired rock and Bora launched scissors.

"Tonight's not my night," Bora admitted.

After a tied round, Changsoo ended up defeating Bora on the third go.

"Looks like I'm driving," Bora said, pocketing the car keys.

My mind flashed back to the last time Bora had driven me and I grimaced.

"It's quite a long drive..." I said cautiously.

Bora pouted. "Don't you trust me?"

"No. Not really."

Jinseung frowned. "Ugh...you're right. I don't trust her either."

"Just let me drive then," Changsoo said. "Like I said before, I'm fine with it."

"All that for nothing," Bora grumbled.

"Don't complain. You get to have a drink now," Jinseung said, nudging a glass of soju towards her.

We clinked glasses and downed our first shot.

"Ahhhh…" Jinseung held his head back in pleasure. "Let's order the steak. I'm starving."

He called the waiter over and we placed our orders. Contrary to Jinseung's insistence that I order the most expensive thing, I decided not to be too greedy. Besides, I'd have to keep my weight in check now that I had been fitted for wardrobe.

Jinseung refilled my shot glass. "Drink up."

"Thanks." I tipped it back. The alcohol warmed my throat and made my head fuzzy. All my earlier worries about my acting seemed to dissolve.

Our steaks arrived shortly, perfectly cooked and succulent, with a heaped side of steamed vegetables. My mouth watered.

Jinseung peered at my plate. "*Aigoo*. Yours is so small. Have some more." He cut off a piece of his steak and put it on my plate.

"It's plenty for me, but thank you."

Partway through our meals, two young women approached our table.

"Excuse me, aren't you Shin Jinseung?" one of them asked.

Jinseung's face reddened. "Uh, yes. It's me." He shifted uncomfortably.

"I love you!" the woman gushed.

"Can we get a photo with you?" the other woman asked.

"Yes. That's fine," Jinseung said.

He stood up and posed between the two women. Bora snapped the photo for them.

After that, Changsoo politely, but firmly, asked them to leave, and the two women sheepishly retreated.

Word spread around the restaurant like wildfire, and Jinseung found himself having to dish out several autographs and photos. I admired the way he got on with it with a smile.

"Sorry about that. I can't usually eat out in peace, unfortunately," Jinseung said, returning to finish his meal.

"No need to apologise. It's all part of being a celebrity," Changsoo said.

"You're so good to your fans," Bora said, dreamy-eyed. "Such a gentleman."

After we finished eating, Jinseung paid the bill and we returned to the car.

"Thanks for the meal, Actor-nim!" Bora said.

"Thanks, *Seonbae-nim*," I echoed, certain he had shouted dinner to try and cheer me up.

"My pleasure," Jinseung said.

Bora looked at her phone. "*Omo*. Tomorrow's call sheet has come through."

"What does it say?"

"You're required all day again, Actor Shin. Actor Chloe… you're not needed."

Jinseung nudged me with his elbow. "That will give you some time to practice," he said. "Your next scene will probably be the one with me in it, so you better not mess up, okay?"

Even though I knew he was just winding me up, I felt a surge of emotion bubble up and spill over, and I couldn't hold back my tears.

15

I still hadn't recovered from my mortification at crying in front of Jinseung when he called me out of the blue the next day.

"It's me, Shin Jinseung," he said. "Intern gave me your number."

Stunned to hear his voice, I found myself unable to speak.

"Are you there?" he asked.

"Yes," I squeaked. "Can I help you with something?" *Please don't bring up the crying incident*, I prayed.

"What are you doing tomorrow night?"

The question took me by surprise. "Tomorrow night? Nothing I can think of…"

"Would you be interested in attending an acting workshop with me? There's one I sometimes go to."

"Uh—"

"I mean, you don't have to. I just thought it might help with your confidence."

"I'll come."

"Really? Great. I'll send you the details."

He hung up before I could say anything else.

An acting workshop…I wondered what it would involve, and more pressingly, why Jinseung wanted me to go with him. *He must feel sorry for me*, I decided, sighing.

———

Is this the right place? I peered at the nondescript door tucked between a convenience store and a cosmetics retailer. After a moment's hesitation, I pushed open the door and entered a dark stairwell. Faint voices drifted down the stairs from the floor above.

I ascended the steps and arrived in a bright studio with floor-to-ceiling mirrors lining the walls. A small group of people sat chatting amongst themselves on the wooden floor. My eyes met Jinseung's and a warm grin spread across his face causing my heart to flutter involuntarily. I even forgot my embarrassment at crying in front of him the other day.

"You made it!" he said.

"Of course." I plopped down next to him. "Did you think I wouldn't come?"

"I couldn't be certain."

"Well, I figured you're right that I need to work on my confidence. Thanks for inviting me."

"No problem."

"What's the workshop about anyway?"

"Portraying emotions."

"Emotions, huh? Sounds useful."

A few minutes later, a boisterous man entered the studio. "Welcome, welcome. Lots of people today. I see some new faces. My name's Lee Hoon and I'm leading today's workshop.

Newbies, could you please stand up and introduce yourselves?"

I stood up along with two others.

A tall, beautiful girl spoke first. "I'm Do Soomi. I'm an actor and model with Kyss Entertainment."

"I'm Kim Inho," the other person, a young man said. "I'm currently a student at Seoul University. I want to take up acting."

Everyone turned their heads to me expectantly. I cleared my throat. "My name's Chloe Gibson. I'm from the UK and soon I'll be appearing in a K-drama."

"Wonderful to have you here," Hoon said. "I hope you'll get a lot out of today's workshop. If you didn't know, today we're focusing on emotions. First, as a warmup, we're going to play a little game. If you've played charades before, it's just like that, but you have to guess the emotion. Who wants to go first?"

Several hands shot up, including Jinseung's.

"Shin Jinseung? All right, you're up."

Jinseung stood up in front of the group. Hoon shuffled a stack of index cards and presented the top card to him. Jinseung squinted at it, thought for a moment, then the left corner of his lip turned up into a smile.

"You're not allowed to say anything," Hoon reminded him.

Jinseung mimed a wide-eyed, mouth-gaping look of shock.

The group of actors called out their guesses.

"Awe?"

"Shock?"

"Terror?"

"Fright?"

The guesses kept coming until someone said, "Horror," which was the correct answer.

Hoon picked the person to go next. Round after round, the game continued. Some emotions were more difficult to guess than others and some acting attempts were so hilarious that guessing paused until the fits of laughter subsided.

I pulled the next card on my turn. Heat rushed to my cheeks at the sight of the word. *Lust*. I froze, stuck at a complete loss as to how to act it out.

"Give it a go," Hoon urged.

Jinseung mouthed words of encouragement.

All eyes on me, I took a deep breath and shoved my embarrassment aside. I narrowed my eyes and bit my lip in the most lustful way I could muster.

Silence reigned. *How long will I have to keep this up?* I wondered.

"Hungry?" someone eventually guessed.

I shook my head. *Not even close.*

"Curious?" someone else ventured.

They'll never guess correctly at this rate. I had no choice but to take it further. I licked my lips seductively and twirled my hair around my finger.

Someone started to giggle, and it set off a chain reaction of laughter. I blushed even harder.

"Horny?" Jinseung asked.

Hearing him say that made me momentarily forget what I was doing, and I dropped my act.

"Sexy?" someone else said. "Is that an emotion?"

My attention snapped back to the game. They were getting close now. I pointed at her and nodded, letting her know she's on the right track.

Several more guesses rapidly ensued, each a variation of sexy or horny.

"Lust?" someone finally guessed.

"Yes!" I said, relieved. I collapsed onto the floor next to Jinseung. "God, that was embarrassing."

"Is that your sex face?" Jinseung teased. "If it is, I'm horrified."

I shoved him. "Shut up."

After the warmup, Hoon announced our first exercise. "Get into pairs, everyone. We're going to improvise some scenes."

Jinseung latched on to me. "Let's do this together."

I nodded enthusiastically. At least I wouldn't have to stand up by myself this time. I could feel more confident with Jinseung by my side.

Hoon went around handing out bits of paper with different scenarios written down.

"A lovers' quarrel," Jinseung said, reading ours.

We had no time to prepare at all.

Hoon called up the first pair to perform their scene, which was "Friends reuniting."

The pair acted out an airport scene, one of them arriving back after living abroad. They expressed their sheer joy at seeing each other again with hugging and crying.

Hoon stopped them after a few minutes and provided feedback, then he invited everyone else to comment.

Jinseung volunteered us to go next. My mind was blank as I stood up with him. Fortunately, Jinseung spoke first, setting up the scene. "Please don't leave me! I beg you. I'll do anything you want." His voice shook.

I crossed my arms and said the first response to enter my head. "It's too late. I've given you so many chances and every time you let me down."

"I'm sorry. I'm so sorry."

The desperation in his voice made me waver for a second, but then I shook my head. "I have to go. I can't do this any longer." I pulled an invisible bag over my shoulder and turned to leave. I took one step before Jinseung pulled me forcefully into a tight back hug, his arms around me, his body against mine. I fell out of character at once. All I could think about was how close we were and how nice it felt.

"Please don't go," he pleaded, then lips to my ear and with a voice soft and smooth as velvet he said, "I love you."

If he wasn't holding on to me, I would have melted to the floor in a puddle. I tried to speak but I could only stutter. "I…I…"

Jinseung kept hugging me until Hoon told us to stop. After that, the rest of the workshop was a blur. I didn't snap out of my stupor until the cold night air hit me when we left the studio.

"Did you have fun?" Jinseung asked.

"Yeah. I had a good time. We really covered a lot, and *seonsaeng-nim* gave us tons of great feedback," I said.

"You can come back any time. KAM will cover the expense since it will help your acting. I already told Changsoo *Hyung*."

"Thanks. I'll definitely go again."

"How are you getting home?"

"I'll take the subway."

"Okay. Well, enjoy the rest of your evening."

"You too. Goodnight."

"Night night."

We parted ways.

On the subway home, I mentally listed the reasons why I shouldn't fall for Jinseung.

1. We work together.
2. He's famous.
3. KAM wouldn't allow us to date.

4. "The dating curse."
5. I might not be able to stay in Korea.
6. Why would he be interested in me anyway?

No. The reasons were clear. I absolutely could not fall for Jinseung. I shouldn't even entertain the idea.

16

"I'm disappointed in you."

Those were my mother's first words when she called me.

After skirting around the issue for a long time, I had no choice but to come clean with everything that had happened. Mum had been asking direct questions about what the school was like, and I couldn't lie to her.

"I'm sorry," I said.

"If you were having trouble in Korea, you should have let me know straight away," she continued. "It breaks my heart that you didn't think to confide in me."

I knew she would react like this. That's why I had been putting off telling her. But I couldn't avoid the subject forever.

"What could you have done to help? I only wanted to save you the worry," I said.

"I would have taken the next plane to Seoul and stayed with you while we sorted everything out."

"Well, I appreciate the thought, but you didn't have to do that. I'm not a little kid anymore. I can take care of myself."

As I said those words, doubt tugged at my mind. *Can I really take care of myself? What would have happened if Seo Minjung hadn't found me drunk and alone on the street?*

My mother exhaled a deep sigh. "You're okay. I suppose that's all that matters."

"I got my money back too."

"Have you spoken to the police?"

"No. I haven't had time."

"Well, I'm going to file a report on your behalf then. Those people should be punished for this."

"Thanks. It's not something I want to deal with right now. There's so much going on."

"I can imagine. Look after yourself, all right? I don't know exactly what being in a K-drama involves, but I don't want you to get taken advantage of again. If it all gets too much for you, come back home, okay?"

"Okay." Truthfully, going back home to the UK was very far from my mind. I had come to Korea to escape my life there. Nothing short of disaster would pull me back.

"Well, call me again soon. I want you to tell me *everything* from now on."

"Yes, Mum."

"Goodnight."

"Goodnight."

———

Immediately after our phone call, Mum set about hiring a lawyer to help us pursue a case against the culprits from SK-Teach. She kept me in the loop by cc-ing me in on her lengthy emails. As she dealt with that, I spent my time job hunting. Too bad that jobs with enough flexibility to work around my part-time acting gig didn't seem to exist. Feeling defeated, my job-hunting efforts dried up after a few days, and I dedicated myself to practicing acting instead—and watching K-dramas (It's research!).

Then, out of the blue, I was summoned for my next scene.

Changsoo dropped me and Jinseung off at the filming location on an overcast afternoon. Large detached houses and evergreen trees lined the charming suburban street. A section of the road had been cordoned off for filming, and several trucks and trailers were parked up on side streets.

Jinseung and I reported to separate trailers to get changed into our costumes before reconvening at hair and makeup.

When we emerged from the trailer, the crew was setting up on the street. The sun still shone in the sky, and filming wouldn't begin until nightfall. A production assistant directed us to one of the houses on the street.

"Im Nara's friend owns this house and she has allowed us to use its facilities while we shoot," she explained.

We walked a path across the lawn to a two-storey house, picture-perfect with its cream weatherboard exterior and burnt-orange-coloured roof. Inside, shoes were piled up on the shelves by the door. We added our shoes to the pile and ventured farther into the house.

The wooden floorboards creaked below us as we navigated the hallway to the lounge where a group of crew members lingered. Changsoo and Bora were seated there too, their laptops open, catching up on work.

Changsoo looked up, spotting us. "All ready for the shoot?"

"Yes. We're just waiting for the sun to go down, then we'll start," Jinseung said.

Changsoo looked out the window. "Shouldn't be much longer…"

"How are you feeling, Actor-nim?" Bora asked me.

"I've had more time to prepare, so I feel more confident this time. Plus, it doesn't seem as difficult as my last scene."

"And you'll be with Actor Shin. He'll help you."

"You're right."

"Don't rely on me too much," Jinseung teased.

Waiting for the sky to darken, we used the time to practice our lines together. Fortunately, I had memorised them off by heart.

As the last rays of sunlight faltered, a crew member called us back outside.

Coldness encroached us. Standing on the side of the road, Jinseung did star jumps to keep warm. I couldn't do the same in my tight miniskirt, but I had a long coat covering me which I pulled tighter.

"I'm so ready for this," Jinseung said, still jumping around.

"You're all hyped up," I said, amused.

He switched to jogging on the spot. "A bit of movement is good for the endorphins. You should try it."

"Really?" I joined in, although my range of movement was limited.

Jinseung began to punch the air, moving from foot to foot. I mimicked him, then he started play fighting with me—a pretend boxing match, which had me in a fit of laughter. Suddenly he launched a crescent kick at me.

"Hey, no fair. I can't kick in this skirt."

"I don't play fair," Jinseung taunted.

A crew member broke up our fight. "We're going to run through the first part of the scene. You need to take your places."

She directed me to my starting place farther up the footpath, while Jinseung made his way to the black sedan parked on the road surrounded by several crew members waiting for him.

I felt my nerves rise in my stomach, but I swallowed them back down.

Following a dry run-through of the scene, recording began.

I walked down the footpath, hands stuffed in my coat pockets. The biting cold made me shiver, serving to disguise my nervous trembling. I aimed to appear as though I were lost in thought.

Jinseung drove the car up to me, pulled over, and wound the window down. "Louise," he said, reaching his head out of the window.

I stopped in my tracks. "Officer Park."

"It's late. What are you doing walking around by yourself?" he asked, voice laced with concern.

"I just finished my shift. I'm heading home."

"You're not driving?"

"My car's out of action. It's being repaired."

"Then let me give you a ride home."

"Really? Is that okay?"

"Of course. It's my job to make sure everyone stays safe in this neighbourhood. Hop in."

I opened the passenger door and got in. Jinseung started driving again, just a short distance, then put the car into park.

"We stop here," he said. "Good job."

I exhaled with relief. One take down. "I must be getting the hang of it."

Filming continued from the top, shooting from another angle. Multiple takes later, Im Nara declared that we'd move on to shooting inside the car. As the crew set up, Jinseung and I were allowed a short break.

"That went much better than I expected," I said.

"You did great! I'm impressed," Jinseung said.

"Are you just saying that? You can tell me the truth. I won't cry again, I promise."

"No. I sincerely mean it."

I still didn't quite believe him, but it was enough to instill me with a smidgeon more confidence.

Bora scurried towards us, bearing two travel mugs filled with hot coffee.

"You're amazing," Jinseung said, eagerly accepting one.

Bora blushed profusely, momentarily forgetting about me until I cleared my throat.

"Here's yours," she said.

"Thank you!" I sipped the coffee down, delighting in the warmth spreading through my body.

Several sips later, we were herded back to the car, which now resided within a low trailer, towed by a small truck.

"So this is how a car scene gets filmed…" I mused, examining the set-up with intrigue.

"Yeah. It's pretty hard to do a dialogue scene in the car and drive at the same time, so they just tow the car along," Jinseung explained. "The camera operator shoots while standing along the side of the trailer."

"Fascinating…"

When instructed to do so, we entered the car. As I pulled on my seatbelt, something caught my eye in the rear-view mirror. I jumped in fright, but quickly realised it was just the sound guy hiding in the back seat.

"Hello," he said. "Don't mind me."

I caught my breath again.

Filming began and the car moved forward. It felt so strange. Jinseung grasped the steering wheel as if he were really driving. Alone together in the car (with the sound guy tucked away out of sight), the scene felt very intimate. I could even ignore the cameraman pointing his lens at us.

"Are you okay?" Jinseung asked, glancing at me.

"It's been a long night." I sighed.

"It must be tiring…"

"Yeah. But I can't complain. What about you? Are you on patrol tonight?"

Jinseung nodded.

We continued to act the scene as the truck towed us in a loop around the block. After each loop, we'd reshoot the scene.

Partway through one take, spits of rain started splashing on the windscreen. A few seconds later, the sky opened up and raindrops pelted down on the car with incredible force. The cameraman desperately tried to shield his equipment from the rain.

"Ah, crap," the sound guy said, removing himself from his hiding place. "We'll have to stop the shoot. Hopefully they already caught enough material."

The crew ran around outside taking equipment under shelter.

"The rain isn't letting up. Shall we run for it?" Jinseung asked.

"Okay."

"On the count of three. One…two…three."

We simultaneously exited the car. Side by side, we ran to the house.

This reminds me of something…

We arrived at the doorstep of the house, soaked and panting. I watched Jinseung as he struggled to catch his breath.

Images flooded back to me—Jinseung's kiss scene where he ran for shelter with Choi Miyoung and they kissed under the eaves of a temple…I realised I was still staring at him. He looked back at me with a bemused expression on his face. I quickly turned away, blushing.

Drenched, we entered the house and removed our wet shoes and coats. Fortunately, the rest of my costume remained reasonably dry. We traipsed down the hallway, careful not to drip water behind us.

Everyone had gathered in the lounge, huddling around Im Nara who was preparing to make an announcement.

"We have decided to wrap up the shoot tonight," she said. "I believe that we shot enough footage to make the scene work, but if an issue arises in editing, a reshoot might be necessary. We'll keep you informed."

A woman who stood by Im Nara's side spoke. "Good effort today, everyone. I've been on set to observe, and I was so impressed with the shoot. I can't wait to see the first episode."

"Who's that?" I whispered to Changsoo.

"Kim Eunsook," he answered.

The name sounded familiar, but I couldn't remember from where. She was an older woman, petite with long black hair. She had a shrewd look in her eyes.

"She's the writer," Bora explained.

To my surprise, Kim Eunsook approached me.

"I don't believe we've been introduced. I'm Kim Eunsook, writer of Hidden History."

"Nice to meet you, Writer-nim. I'm Chloe Gibson."

"Are you really a first-time actor?"

"Yes."

"*Aigoo*. I can't believe it! You did so well."

"Thank you," I croaked.

"Can I speak with you and Shin Jinseung for a minute? There are some script changes I'd like to discuss."

"Of course."

We relocated to the dining room. Kim Eunsook sat opposite me and Jinseung at the table.

"I've decided to change part of the storyline from episode three going forward," she explained. "This involves the character Louise."

I snapped to attention, wondering what she had planned for my character.

17

"An email will be going out tomorrow," Eunsook said. "But I thought I'd let both of you know in person, since I'm here."

"So what are the changes?" I asked, voice tinged with concern.

"Don't worry, it's nothing bad," she reassured me. "In fact, quite the opposite. You see, I was going to have Louise killed off in the third episode, but recently I've had second thoughts. Seeing your scene together tonight made it even more clear to me… I don't want to kill Louise."

"So, Louise will live?"

"She will live…but she will go missing. Once Officer Park and Detective Jung solve the case, she'll return."

"I see."

"You won't be required for too many extra scenes, just in the last couple of episodes when you make your reappearance."

"What changed your mind?" Jinseung asked.

Eunsook broke into a sheepish smile. "I like the Louise and

Officer Park pairing too much, and I think the fans will too. That's why I want them to reunite at the end."

Jinseung chuckled. "So that's why."

"You two have great chemistry!"

Jinseung wiggled his eyebrows at me.

"Stop that!" I said, batting him away.

Eunsook laughed. "Too cute!"

———

A couple days later, three new scripts arrived at KAM for me to pick up—the amended third episode script, plus the scripts for the fourth and fifth episodes.

The KAM lobby bustled with busy employees. I watched a digital screen display a photo of Jinseung in a relaxed pose upon a couch, his shirt halfway undone, and a come-hither look in his eyes. My jaw gaped at the sight. *I can't believe I work with this gorgeous human…*

A voice came from behind me. "Actor Chloe?"

I swung around, startled.

It was Seo Minjung. She looked immaculate as usual, with her sleek low ponytail and beautifully tailored skirt suit.

"What brings you here? No filming today?" she asked.

I nodded. "No filming for me. I'm here to pick up some new scripts."

"Do you know where they were delivered?"

"Shin Jinseung's management office."

"I'll get them for you."

"Thanks!"

"Do you have time for a catch-up? Wait for me in the cafeteria and I'll buy you a coffee."

"That sounds great."

"Okay. I'll be back in a minute." Minjung dashed to the elevator.

I made my way to the staff cafeteria situated down the right end of the lobby. I took a seat at an empty table.

Minjung returned shortly, a thick pile of scripts tucked beneath her arm. "I hope you don't mind, but I had a quick flick through. I couldn't help it. It's so gripping. Writer-nim is truly excellent."

"I don't mind. I'm eager to read it too."

While Minjung ordered the coffee, I scanned my eyes over the scripts, looking for parts which involved Louise. I stuffed them in my bag when Minjung returned.

She pulled out a chair. "So, tell me everything. What's it like to act in a drama?"

I relayed my experience so far while we sipped the strong coffee. She listened intently, keen to hear every detail.

I was describing what it was like to act alongside Shin Jinseung when my phone started ringing—a call from an unsaved number.

"Go ahead, take it," Minjung said.

I swiped to accept the call. "*Yeoboseyo?*"

"Chloe Gibson?" a female voice asked.

"Yes."

"This is Baek Yena."

Baek Yena? Why would she call me? How does she even have my number? "Baek Yena!" I exclaimed, my voice breaking.

Minjung's mouth dropped open.

"Don't sound so shocked!" Yena said. "I got your number from Shin Jinseung's manager. I'm having a party at my house next week, and I wanted to invite a select few people from Hidden History. I thought of you and Shin Jinseung. What do you think?"

"Absolutely! I'll come."

I simply couldn't pass up an opportunity like this.

"Wonderful! I'll text you the details."

Still in a state of awe, I put my phone away.

"Baek Yena called you?" Minjung asked, gobsmacked.

"I'm surprised too. She invited me to a party at her place."

"*Omo*. That's so cool. I'm jealous."

"She's inviting Shin Jinseung as well."

"Exciting! What will you wear? How will you do your makeup?"

"I don't know!"

Minjung appeared more frantic than me.

A party at Baek Yena's place…I wonder what it will be like.

A text message from Yena came through shortly. "Join me for a casual dinner party," it read, followed by the address and timing.

"When is it?" Minjung asked.

"Next Friday."

"Let me see if I can arrange a stylist and something to wear through KAM. It's a business expense, right? This is a networking opportunity for you."

"Oh, really? That would be amazing if possible. It's just a casual event, though, so nothing too extravagant."

"I'll see what I can do."

Minjung seemed just as excited as I was. She saw me off, promising to do everything she could to help me look my best on the day.

As I rode the subway home, my phone buzzed.

Jinseung: Hi Chloe. Are you going to Baek Yena's
  party? Want to go together?
Chloe: Yes. Let's go 😊

Jinseung: It's a date!

A date?! I shook my head, telling myself it was just a turn of phrase.

18

F ace up close to my bathroom mirror, I touched up my lips with a thin layer of moisturising lipstick in a colour called Rouge Royale, which promised to be long-wearing and "kiss-proof". I pouted, admiring how juicy and kissable my lips looked. Not that I ever imagined I'd be kissed by anyone that night. That would be completely delusional. *Who would kiss me anyway? Shin Jinseung?* I scoffed.

I had already had my makeup done. Minjung had arranged a stylist and loaned me some designer clothes from KAM's extensive closet. I wore a black turtleneck beneath a slip dress with a leather jacket over the top. The combination looked very chic.

I was trying on different pairs of earrings when I received a text message.

Jinseung: Are you ready? I'm in the taxi outside.

I quickly settled on a pair of dangly silver earrings, grabbed my purse, and dashed to the elevator.

A fancy black cab with tinted windows awaited me at the entrance. A uniformed driver got out and opened the door for me.

I slipped into the leather interior next to Jinseung. He wore slim black pants and a chunky wool sweater with a white shirt collar poking out underneath. A pair of thick-framed glasses and a black face mask hid his features. He pulled the mask down to speak. "Why, hello there. Nice threads."

"Thanks. They're actually on loan from KAM."

"Ah…You've discovered one of many work perks."

"Thanks for taking me to the party."

"That's all right. I thought it might be kind of intimidating if you arrived by yourself. I'm sure you're not used to being around lots of celebrities. I think it will mainly be people from Hidden History, but still…"

"You're right. I'm really excited to go, but a bit nervous as well. I don't have much in common with celebrities."

"Well, you look the part anyway. And who knows? Once the drama starts to air, maybe you'll get a little bit famous."

I laughed. "No way."

"Why not?"

"I'm not even a real actor."

"*Aigoo*. Your acting looked real to me."

"You know what I mean."

Jinseung folded his arms. "Sounds like you've got a pretty serious case of imposter syndrome."

"Imposter syndrome?"

"Despite your success, you feel like a fraud. Take it from me, you need to get out of that mindset. It takes up far too much energy."

"Perhaps."

"Trust me. Have more self-confidence. And let me tell you

something, I've worked with many 'real' actors who weren't half as good as you."

"Really?"

Jinseung nodded.

I sighed. "I guess you're right. My mindset isn't doing me any favours." I ran a hand through my hair, ruminating on Jinseung's advice. He had certainly given me some food for thought.

"Oh—" Jinseung said, his eyes on me.

"What?"

"Your earring fell out."

I felt my earlobes. The right earring was missing. "Where did it go?" I looked around, then spotted it in my lap, light glinting off its edges. I tried to put it back in but struggled without a mirror.

Jinseung reached towards me. "Here, let me."

He took the earring and moved closer. He brushed my hair back behind my ear. With a focused expression on his face, he threaded the earring into my lobe, still holding my hair back, his hand against my neck. I could feel his warm breath against my cheek, making my skin prickle.

"There," he said, leaning back to admire his handiwork.

"Thanks."

The taxi slowed upon entering a posh neighbourhood with enormous mansions lining the streets. The driver dropped us off outside a four-storey house, modern and minimalist in design, with a flat roof and each floor jutting out at different angles creating the illusion of a stack of boxes. The lights were on inside and jazz music drifted from an open window.

"Wow. Baek Yena lives here?" I said, as we approached the house. "Impressive."

"I wonder who designed her house. Some famous architect, I suspect," Jinseung said.

We ascended the stairs leading up the side of the house to the entrance.

Jinseung pressed the doorbell. The door clicked open shortly, and a young woman neatly dressed in black pants and a white shirt greeted us.

"The guests are in the lounge. This way, please," she guided us down the hallway.

The interior of the house had a lived-in feel. Framed artwork covered the walls—a mixture of professional pieces and what looked like kids' artwork. Stacks of worn books and vinyls overflowed shelves and took up residence on the floor and in boxes. I spied a family photo of Baek Yena, her husband, and her three young children, huddled together and smiling broadly. They looked like the perfect family.

We entered the vast lounge area, possessing beautiful views over park-like surroundings. A gas fireplace burned, and couches were arranged to maximise potential interaction between their occupants.

Guests sat on the couches and on cushions on the floor. Others stood in corners partaking in intimate one-on-one conversations.

I recognised most of the people there from Hidden History —actors, plus Im Nara and Kim Eunsook, but there were also a few unfamiliar faces.

"Chloe, Jinseungie!" Baek Yena waved us over to join them. She grabbed more cushions and signalled for us to sit down. "Did you two come together?"

"Yes," Jinseung said.

"That's so sweet! I'm glad you could make it."

"Hey, I'm Ko Dongwoo." the man sitting next to her said. He had long hair and rugged features. "I'm Yena's husband."

Other people around us also introduced themselves.

Before long, I had a glass of wine in my hand, and I was chatting away with several people—forgetting all about the fact that they were celebrities. An endless stream of canapés flowed from the kitchen, and my wine glass seemed to get refilled whenever I wasn't looking. I had to make a concerted effort to drink slowly.

Kim Eunsook and Baek Yena started gushing over how cute Jinseung and I looked together.

"It's like magic," Kim Eunsook said. "So little time together and you've already managed to achieve such good on-screen chemistry."

"And off-screen as well," Baek Yena jibed, lightly elbowing Jinseung.

"What's that for?" Jinseung asked, bemused.

"How on earth did PD-nim manage to find you at such short notice?" Kim Eunsook asked me.

"Well, it's actually a funny story." I relayed the whole tale of how I had been conned, and how Seo Minjung spotted me on the street at my lowest point.

"*Aigoo*. That's crazy."

"And here's the kicker," Jinseung said. "It wasn't my first time meeting Chloe."

"What do you mean?"

"I came to Korea as a teenager," I explained. "I did a high school exchange."

"The same high school that I attended," Jinseung continued.

Baek Yena gasped. "*Omo!* It's like you were destined to be brought back together."

Kim Eunsook seemed struck by a sudden idea. "Why don't you get KAM to write up a press release about this? The media would love it! It could drum up some interest in the drama too."

"That's not a bad idea." Jinseung turned to me. "What do you think?"

"Sure. I don't mind."

"Then it's settled. I'll ask Changsoo *Hyung* to organise it."

"There's going to be so much interest in this story!" Kim Eunsook said excitedly.

———

As the night wore on, the guests grew increasingly intoxicated —especially Baek Yena. She turned the music up and started dancing with her husband who didn't seem overly enthusiastic.

I had become separated from Jinseung, but Kim Eunsook took me under her wing as we talked and snapped photographs with various guests.

When Baek Yena tired of dancing she bounded towards me and pulled me aside.

"Guess what…" she said in a conspiratorial tone.

"What?"

"You and Shin Jinseung…"

"Yes?"

"…Have to kiss!"

Facepalm. "I know that! I've read the script."

She sidled up to me. "So…are you nervous about it?"

"Yeah, I guess so. More embarrassed than anything. I haven't even kissed a guy in real life for a long time, and now I have to kiss on-screen."

Kim Jaehyun, who had been nearby, slid into our private conversation.

"I've done plenty of kiss scenes in my day," he said. "I'd be willing to let you practice on me."

"Why would she practice with you? Dirty old man," Baek Yena snapped back.

"Who are you calling old?"

"So you don't deny that you're dirty?"

"Well, there's no denying that."

"She should practice the scene with Shin Jinseung. Hey! Jinseungie!"

Jinseung, who stood at the opposite end of the room, turned his head to us, eyebrows raised.

Baek Yena gestured for him to come over, a scheming look on her face.

He cautiously approached. "What is it?"

"Show Chloe how to kiss."

"What?" he spluttered.

"The kiss scene. You don't want it to look awkward, so you should practice and get comfortable with it."

"That's really not necessary…" I said, holding my hands out in protest.

Jinseung stroked his chin. "Should we?"

"Huh?" I squeaked.

"It's not a bad idea."

"Well…"

"See? He agrees," Baek Yena said. "You can use an empty bedroom if you like."

Is she serious? I suddenly felt very hot and flustered.

"I'm joking!" Baek Yena said.

"They'll work it out in their own time," Kim Jaehyun assured her.

"That's right," Jinseung said. He turned to me. "You have nothing to worry about."

"Oh! I love this song!" Baek Yena's attention snapped away and she resumed dancing, targeting an unsuspecting Im Nara.

I regained my composure in her absence. "I wonder what that was all about…"

Jinseung scratched his head. "Well, Baek Yena seems to think that we'd make a good couple. I don't know where she got that idea from, but she won't stop bugging me about it."

"*Aigoo*…"

Ko Dongwoo had overheard us talking. "Sorry about that. It's her hobby to play cupid. Either play along or just ignore it. She's harmless, really."

"Ah. That's good to know," Jinseung said.

———

Midnight drew near. Some of the party guests had already left, returning home to their families, or to get some much-needed sleep before busy schedules ahead. I had stopped drinking a long time ago, and the drunken antics of the remaining guests ceased to be all that amusing.

"Do you want to leave soon?" Jinseung asked. He must have sensed my rising boredom.

"Yeah. I think I will."

"Then I'll go too. I'll order a taxi."

"Are you sure? You can stay if you want."

"I'd rather leave with you."

I wasn't sure whether he genuinely wanted to leave, or if he was just being a gentleman, but I was happy either way.

We said our goodbyes to Baek Yena. She protested, but eventually resigned herself to the fact that we were leaving.

The taxi arrived and we clambered inside.

"So, what did you think? Was it all that you imagined it would be?" Jinseung asked.

"I had fun."

"Everyone seems to like you."

"I'm relieved."

"…I'm actually not that tired. Are you?"

"No. Not particularly."

He seemed to be angling at something.

I realised the taxi was heading towards the KAM office, rather than my apartment.

"Do you need to get something from the office?" I asked.

"Actually, I thought I might use a practice room."

"At this time of night?"

"Yeah. It wouldn't be the first time."

"Then…should I join you?"

Jinseung nodded. "That scene…it could be shot any day now."

"The kiss scene?"

"Yes. *That* scene. We haven't done any work on it apart from a dry read-through. I meant what I said before. It wouldn't be a bad idea to practice it properly."

My heart rate increased. *Does he mean it? Is he drunk or something?*

"So you…want to practice the kiss?" I asked.

He nodded.

19

"This is the part where we kiss," Jinseung reminded me.

I had said my line and then frozen, overwhelmed by the prospect of having to launch myself towards him and press my lips to his.

"Oh. Right," I mumbled.

We stood together in a small, windowless practice room at KAM, possibly the only two people in the entire building. The air was so quiet and still, making me hyperaware of Jinseung's movements, the sound of his breath, and his scent—slightly sweet, a little bit sweaty.

"You have to take the lead on this," Jinseung pushed. "Louise kisses Officer Park, not the other way around."

"All right. Got it."

"Let's try again."

We started from the top, where Louise gets out of the car and Officer Park reprimands her for her crazy driving. He wants to know if something's wrong.

"I...can't say anything," I said.

"Don't be scared. Tell me," he urged.

"I…"

He stood patiently, watching me, waiting for me to do something.

My heart hammered in my chest. I took a deep breath. *Okay…Let's do this*. I closed in on him, tilted my head, and gently pressed my mouth up against his, my lips sealed tight. I didn't dare take it any further. I held the kiss for a moment before breaking away, then I looked at him expectantly.

He raised his eyebrow. "Was that it?"

I frowned. "How should I do it then?"

"Well…how should I put this? I don't think the kiss should be too polite. Louise needs to throw Officer Park off-guard, making him completely flustered so he forgets everything."

"So, I need to kiss you…*harder?*"

"Yes. And you're too stiff. Don't clench your mouth shut. Move a little bit."

*Oh my gosh…*My cheeks blazed with embarrassment. "Can you show me?"

Before I could mentally prepare myself, Jinseung flung himself at me and pushed my mouth open with his lips, eliciting a gasp I couldn't hold back. He moved his lips against mine, softly but purposefully. I didn't take a breath until he pulled away.

"More like that," he explained.

"I'll try to."

"Don't be shy, okay? You don't have to hold back with me."

"Right. Umm…What should I do with my hands?"

Jinseung thought for a moment, then he took my left hand and pulled it up to his shoulder, then my right hand to the side of his neck.

"Like this," he said. "I think that will look good."

"Okay."

"Now, let's try it again. This time you have to take the lead."

We positioned ourselves and ran through our lines again. I didn't hesitate this time. At my cue, I dove straight into the kiss, with my hand on his neck pulling his head down and making our lips meet.

Jinseung feigned shock but then started to engage, returning the kiss with vigorous enthusiasm. It felt warm and slightly wet.

*Is this real? It feels like a real kiss...*One slip of the tongue and we'd practically be making out.

Jinseung's hand clutched my waist, his fingertips digging in, massaging my lower back. I could feel a vein throbbing in his neck, faster and faster...

Lost in the kiss, I nearly forgot to break away, but Jinseung didn't let up until I remembered and detached myself from his lips.

We both had to take a moment to catch our breath.

"Was that too much?" I asked.

Jinseung shrugged. "I don't think so. But it will be up to PD-nim to decide."

"I hope it looks okay. What if I have a weird expression on my face when I kiss?"

"I'm sure you don't."

"But you couldn't see, could you?"

"Yeah. My eyes were closed. If you're worried about it, we should see what it looks like."

"How can we?"

"Let's record it. There's a tripod around somewhere. It might be in one of the other practice rooms. I'll look for it."

While he left the room to search for the tripod, I took slow breaths, trying to calm myself.

Shin Jinseung kissed me…He really kissed me…So what if he's acting? It didn't feel like acting…

Jinseung reappeared holding a tripod in his arms. He set it up in the corner of the room, balancing his phone on top.

Before we resumed, he took his sweater off, revealing the crumpled white shirt underneath. *So I'm not the only one feeling hot right now…*

We got straight into it. I grabbed onto him and kissed his lips, slowly at first, but building in intensity. Jinseung eagerly responded. He held me closer this time, and I could feel his hard abs up against me. It felt so good that I didn't want to stop, but eventually I had to tear myself away.

Jinseung opened his eyes. He stared at me, biting his lip. My face burned under his gaze.

"The recording," I croaked.

"Right!" He retrieved his phone. "Let's see…"

Standing next to me, he positioned his phone in front of us and played the clip.

I watched with bated breath. There I was, rosy-cheeked, and with a look of concentration on my face as I kissed him. Jinseung's face was more animated, conveying surprise, then delight, and then…*desire?* Anyone who didn't know that he was acting would have thought he was genuinely into it. It looked like a perfectly hot, romantic kiss scene.

"It looks good," Jinseung said, voice slightly hoarse.

"Your face looks so expressive…"

"Viewers love to see emotion."

"Can you send that to me? I want to study it more closely."

"No. It's too risky. I'm going to delete it. It would cause havoc if it somehow leaked out."

"Ah. I understand."

He was right. Something like this could cause a scandal if it ended up in the wrong hands.

He put his phone away in his pocket. "It's getting late. We should go home."

I agreed, even though I didn't feel tired. The kissing had flooded my body with adrenaline.

Jinseung booked a taxi. It arrived outside the building a few minutes later.

Seated in the back of the car, I stroked my lips. They felt puffy and dry. The "kiss-proof" lipstick had completely worn off. I applied a thick layer of balm with my finger and rubbed my lips together. I noticed Jinseung watching me as if hypnotised.

"Sorry if my lips felt dry before," I said.

"No, they felt...nice..." His voice trailed off. "Your seatbelt—"

"Huh? Oh." I had forgot to put it on. I tried to pull it down, but it was jammed.

Jinseung reached across to help, his body inches from mine. He also struggled, but one more try and he was able to ease it down

"There," he said, clicking it into place.

He lingered in front of me, so close that if I leaned forward just a little, our lips would brush. He swallowed, then as if remembering something, he suddenly pulled away.

I slumped in my seat, disappointed. *What was I thinking?* I reminded myself that he had only been acting before, and that he had no reason to kiss me in real life.

I watched the streets of Seoul go by out the window, a blur of colourful lights.

20

"Looking forward to showing everyone what we've been working on?" Jinseung teased with a smirk.

I lightly punched him in retaliation. He gripped his arm and staggered in mock pain.

We occupied a cordoned-off section of road, waiting for our scene to begin. The kiss scene.

The cameraman set up to shoot from the part where Officer Park approaches Louise's car. Jinseung, dressed in police uniform, rocked on his heels as he waited.

Baek Yena watched attentively from the sidelines, laid back on a fold-out chair, sipping bubble tea through a straw. Her manager stood beside her, shading her with a sun umbrella. Bora and Changsoo also watched from nearby.

Thanks to our practice kissing, I didn't feel too nervous about the scene since I knew exactly what to expect. Nevertheless, my heartbeat sped up as our cue drew near.

"Starting positions please," Im Nara said.

I got into the car. Jinseung walked off camera.

"Action."

Jinseung approached my vehicle. I got out, acting irritated.

"Louise, what's gotten into you? Have you been drinking?" he asked.

"No."

"You ran a red light. You're speeding. You're driving erratically. I should give you a ticket."

"I don't have time for this."

Jinseung raised an eyebrow. "…Is everything okay?"

"I…can't say anything."

He softened. "Don't be scared. Tell me."

"I…" I searched his eyes, and then without hesitation, stepped closer, pulled his head down, and kissed his lips, just as we had practiced.

Jinseung acted surprised at first, then he kissed me back with a hungry urgency. It took all my effort to stay focused on acting and not lose myself completely.

Just as the kiss reached its peak, I broke away, and before Jinseung could react, I got back into the car, hit the accelerator, and sped off a short distance down the road. Jinseung watched on, completely dumbstruck, powerless to act.

When I returned for the next take, Bora and Changsoo stared at me, mouths agape.

"What?" I asked.

"That kiss…" Changsoo said, eyes wide.

"How did you do that? It's like you're already used to kissing each other…" Bora said, a hint of suspicion in her voice.

"They must have done a lot of practice," Yena jibed, appearing from nearby having overheard the conversation.

"Practice?" Bora squeaked. "Did you? When?"

"Well…" I said, awkwardly.

Jinseung cut in. "Since this was Chloe's first kiss scene, sharing my expertise was the right thing to do."

"*Omo.* Sharing your expertise?" Bora repeated, stunned.

"I knew it!" Yena said.

———

Thanks to our excellent kissing skills, we were able to wrap up the scene much earlier than anticipated.

"Good work today," Changsoo said, opening the van door.

Jinseung and I climbed in.

"I still can't believe you could kiss like that. Isn't it too risqué for a prime-time drama?" Bora said, pulling her seatbelt on.

"I like to push boundaries," Jinseung retorted.

"When it comes to kiss scenes, Shin Jinseung has a reputation to uphold," Changsoo said. "Don't you remember he won that 'best kiss' award for the scene with Choi Miyoung in Midnight Dreaming?"

"I remember," Bora said. "But still…"

"I'm more impressed that it was Chloe's first kiss scene, and she was able to hit the ball out of the park on the first take."

"I couldn't have done it so well if *Seonbae-nim* hadn't coached me," I admitted.

"Hey, Actor Shin, who's the better kisser, Chloe or Choi Miyoung?" Bora asked.

I shot up in my seat, startled by the intimate question.

"*Aigoo.* Don't ask him that," Changsoo said.

"It's all acting," Jinseung said. "I don't make comparisons like that."

"That's sensible."

"That's boring," Bora grumbled.

Further into the journey home, she finally dropped the subject of kissing and turned her attention to her iPad. "Oh? What's this?"

"What is it?" Changsoo asked.

"An email from Drama Day News. They're requesting an interview with Chloe and Jinseung."

"*Omo*. It must be regarding the press release we sent out."

"Yes. They want to write an article about your high school memories of each other."

"What do you think, Jinseung, Chloe?"

"I'm in," Jinseung said straight away. He nudged me with his elbow. "Up for a trip down memory lane, Chloe?"

My high school memories of Jinseung…Since he had revealed that we went to the same high school, I had racked my brain trying to remember him, but nothing surfaced. Perhaps the interview would help jog my memory? "Yes. I'll do it," I said.

21

A young female journalist from Drama Day News entered the meeting room carrying a thick brown envelope marked *Tongyeong—Important*. I eyed it warily, curious about its contents.

"Hello, I'm Hwang Yura from Drama Day News," she said. "I'm here to conduct the interview." She handed us a business card each.

"Hwang Yura," Jinseung repeated, studying the card. "Shall we get started?"

"Yes. Is it okay if I record?"

"Go ahead."

She set her phone to record audio and placed it in the centre of the table. She kept the brown envelope safely on her lap as she seated herself.

"Chloe Gibson, you were cast in Hidden History after a chance encounter with a KAM talent scout who spotted you on the street," she said. "At what point did you realise you'd be working alongside Shin Jinseung?"

"I found out after I auditioned," I replied.

"And did you recognise him?"

"No, I didn't."

She turned to Jinseung. "Did you recognise her?"

"Yes," he said. "It took me a moment, but then I realised where I'd seen her. I was so shocked. I had never expected to see her again."

"It must have felt like a blast from the past."

"Yeah. It was crazy."

"So, what was Chloe like in high school?"

I blushed, feeling self-conscious about how he would answer. *What does Jinseung remember about me? What was my impression on him?*

"Ummm…well," Jinseung fumbled for words. "She was the only foreigner, so naturally, people were curious about her."

"You too?"

"Yes. Of course."

"Anything else?"

"Her Korean was terrible at first."

"Hey!" I interjected.

"But she seemed to become fluent pretty fast," he added. "She was a high achiever even with Korean as her second language."

"I'm a nerd," I confessed. "Actually, as a foreigner I was excused from having to study after school with the other students, but I still joined in a lot of the time, anyway."

I had been top of my class in my UK high school, but the competitive nature of Korean schooling still came as a shock to my system. I had to study really hard to keep up with everyone, but somehow, I made it work.

"Were you good at studying, Shin Jinseung?" Yura asked.

"No. Not at all," he said. "I barely passed high school. Not that I lacked intelligence, I just wasn't focused on school and had no aspirations to go to university, work a corporate job, anything like that."

"So you knew you wanted to be an actor, then?"

"I wanted to work in entertainment. I actually did idol training but ended up as an actor, not a singer."

I gasped. "You wanted to be an idol?" *This is news to me…*

"You would have made a great idol," Yura said, enthusiastically.

Jinseung rubbed his head, shyly averting his eyes. "You think so? Actually, I'm glad things worked out this way. The idol lifestyle is a bit too full on, I reckon."

"Ah, I can understand that."

The envelope on Yura's lap made a rustling sound.

"I've got something I want to show both of you," she said. "Perhaps it might jog some more memories." She produced the envelope and opened it, pulling out what looked like a magazine, some of its pages bookmarked with sticky tabs.

"What's that?" Jinseung asked.

Yura held it up so we could see.

The words *Tongyeong High School Yearbook 2011* emblazoned its cover.

I gasped. "That's our yearbook!"

"How did you get this?" Jinseung asked.

"I made some calls and found an ex-student who still had it in their possession," Yura replied.

"Can I have a look?"

"Yes. Check out the pages I have bookmarked." She passed it to him.

Jinseung pulled his chair up close to mine so we could both see. He flicked to one of the bookmarked pages. There I was, smiling in a class photo.

Jinseung grinned. "You still look the same."

I ran my finger across the glossy page, scanning the faces of my former classmates. "Yoo Mina…Han Seri…"

"Were you close with them?" Yura asked.

"Yes. We were best friends. We were inseparable, especially me and Seri. My family hosted her when she did an exchange at my intermediate school when we were 13, then her family hosted me when I went to Tongyeong High School. We're practically sisters."

"Have you kept in touch?"

"Yes. We still chat on social media and email…although, not as often as we used to." A hint of regret edged its way into my voice.

"Is she still in Tongyeong?"

"No. She's in Melbourne now, but she planned to return to Korea this year so we could meet." I made a mental note to follow up with her.

Jinseung turned to the next bookmarked page. He smiled. "My old class…"

"Where are you?" I asked. "Oh—" I spotted him.

He appeared slightly chubby, with an awkward bowl-cut hairstyle, caterpillar eyebrows, and a dorky grin, but the same handsome, mischievous face peered out underneath.

"That's you!" I looked closer, blinking as I studied his image. My brain was on the verge of a memory, but the harder I tried to recover it, the more it slipped away. "I think…I think I do remember you…"

"Of course. How could you forget a face like mine?" Jinseung said. "I've lost my baby fat since then, of course."

"Turn to the next bookmark," Yura urged.

Jinseung flipped through the yearbook, stopping at the final bookmark. On a spread titled *Community Service Day*, my eyes fell upon a photograph of a small group of students, Jinseung and I standing side by side, and in the background, a beautiful, sandy beach. The floodgates in my mind opened up, and a deluge of memories poured in.

"I remember this," I said. "I remember this day…"

I let the memory wash over me, transporting me back to that moment eight years ago.

It was a rare break from the usual crushing school day routine of back-to-back lessons and study sessions. Instead, the entire school spent a day doing volunteer work.

We were divided into small groups, mixing up the students from different classes and different year levels. Jinseung and I ended up in the same group. We were assigned the task of clearing litter from a beach.

It was a gloriously hot, sunny summer day. It felt so good to be out in the fresh air, away from the stuffy classroom. None of us minded having to pick up rubbish. But partway through the day, disaster struck…

I had removed my shoes to enjoy the warm sand against my bare feet. Walking along the beach, a piercing pain shot through my foot. The sand turned red with my blood. I shrieked.

It was Jinseung who had rushed to my aid. He asked the teacher looking after our group to bring the first aid kit, then he had tended to my wound himself, removing the shard of glass that had wedged itself in my foot, cleaning and sterilising the cut, and wrapping my foot in bandages.

When the beach cleanup finished, the other students in the group cooled off in the ocean. I couldn't due to my injury, but Jinseung stayed with me on the beach to keep me company.

Snapping back to the present, I turned to Jinseung. "You were really nice to me. Did I ever thank you?"

Jinseung shrugged. "Probably. I don't remember."

"What happened?" Yura asked.

I told her the story, with Jinseung interrupting now and then to add his own embellishments.

"Awww, that's sweet," Yura said. "And did you talk to each other at school after that?"

"No," I confessed.

"I saw her around at school, but we didn't have much of a reason to interact," Jinseung explained. "We weren't in the same year, we didn't have any mutual friends…"

"Ah. I see." Yura asked a few more questions before she began to wrap up the interview. "I have one more question. Do you have any plans to go back to Tongyeong?"

"Yes," I replied. "Part of the reason I came back to Korea was to visit my host family and to see Tongyeong again."

"And you, Shin Jinseung?"

"I would like to see my parents again soon, and my dog, Buster."

"Buster! How cute. Well, that's about everything. Thank you so much for your time today," Yura said.

"No problem."

"I'll send the article through to your manager to review before we hit publish." She got up from the chair, bowed her head, and said goodbye.

I stopped her before she reached the door.

"You forgot this." I picked up the yearbook she had left on the table.

"You can keep it," Yura said. "I've already got everything I need from it."

"Okay. Thanks."

She left the room.

"Do you want this?" I asked Jinseung.

"You can have it. I still have my copy somewhere at my parents' house."

"Thanks. Well, I guess I'll get going then."

"Hey—have you had lunch?"

"No."

"Then let's go to the cafeteria. I have something I want to ask you about."

"Oh? All right then."

Wondering what he had to say to me, I followed Jinseung down to the cafeteria on the ground floor of KAM headquarters.

We grabbed a table, and over bowls of *bibimbap*, Jinseung leaned in to speak.

"Are you really planning to go back to Tongyeong?" he asked.

"Yes," I replied.

"Soon you won't have too many scenes left to shoot. I'm sure you'll have time to go."

"What about you?"

"The pace of filming is only going to increase from now on. Once the first episode airs, I don't think I'll have much time off, so I want to go soon. As soon as possible, actually—if *PD-nim* allows it."

"I should go soon, too. There's no reason to put it off."

"It seems like we're both on the same page, so how about this? Why don't we go together?"

My eyebrows shot up in surprise at his proposal. "Really?"

"Now, I can't guarantee it so don't get your hopes up—"

"I'm not!"

"—but if we can both get a few days off together, let's do it. It would be nice to have company for the journey. I could drive us there. What do you think?"

A road trip with Shin Jinseung? How cool would that be. "I'm in. Let's go to Tongyeong."

22

I should have heeded Jinseung's advice not to get my hopes up. One week after our chat in the KAM cafeteria, I rode a bus from Seoul to Tongyeong, alone.

He had called me the other night, apologetic that he couldn't come. He was required on set on what was supposed to be his day off. I tried to brush my disappointment aside—I could still enjoy the trip without him.

Face pressed to the bus window, I peered out as the picturesque seascape unfolded before me. I had arrived in the beautiful port city of Tongyeong, often called the Napoli of Korea for its attractive seaside charm.

The bus rolled into Tongyeong station. I slung my duffel bag over my shoulder and searched the waiting area for my host parents, Mr. Han and Mrs. Soo. My throat tightened when my eyes met theirs.

Mrs. Soo waved frantically, her eyes crinkling as she smiled, and Mr. Han stood with his arms folded, nodding his wispy-haired head. Both of them looked the same as I remembered, only slightly greyer. Seeing them again brought tears to my eyes. I hadn't realised how much I missed them.

"*Eomeoni! Abeoji!*" I ran to them.

"Chloe!" Mrs. Soo cried.

"My daughter!" Mr. Han called.

I hurtled into their arms.

"*Unnie*," a third voice said.

I turned to see Seri approach from nearby. I leapt back in surprise. "Seri-ya! I didn't know you would be here."

"When I heard you were coming, I expedited my travel plans," she explained.

I hugged her. "Thank you. It's so good to see you."

Seri looked just as pretty as she did in high school, but more mature with shorter, side-parted hair, and light makeup on a thinner, more angular face.

Mr. Han drove us to their house in Inpyeong-dong. I felt faintly nostalgic passing through the city which my sixteen-year-old self once knew intimately.

As we drove up the driveway, a golden retriever ran over to us, barking.

I opened the car door and the dog came over to sniff me, tail wagging with excitement.

"Who's this?" I asked, patting the dog.

"Her name's Snow," Mrs. Soo said. "Oscar is no longer around, I'm afraid. He passed away."

"Yes, Seri told me. I'm very sorry."

Oscar was the family dog when I had lived with them, and I had loved him very much.

"Come inside and have some tea," Mrs. Soo said. "We have a lot of catching up to do."

I followed the family inside the house. The interior hadn't

changed one bit. Faded floral wallpaper lined the walls, and mismatched second-hand furniture stood on creaky wooden floorboards.

We sat on cushions around a low dining table. Mrs. Soo prepared fragrant herbal tea and served it using a traditional Korean celadon tea set.

"So Chloe, you're in a drama with Shin Jinseung and Baek Yena. I can't believe it!" Seri gushed.

"Neither can I," I admitted.

"What happened to teaching English?" Mr. Han asked, brow furrowed beneath his spectacles.

"Things didn't work out. But after I've finished the drama, I might try to get a job teaching again."

"A respectable plan."

"Won't you be able to get more entertainment work?" Mrs. Soo asked.

"I don't think so. The work available to foreigners is pretty limited."

"Oh, I see. Well, whatever happens, I wish you success."

"Thank you. How have things been here? Still working at GNU?" I asked Mr. Han.

"Yes. Still teaching at the university. My wife has a job now too."

"Really?"

"Yes," Mrs. Soo replied. "I'm working part-time at a clothing store. I found myself with more time on my hands after Seri moved out."

"It's good to keep busy. Seri-ya, how's Melbourne?"

"It's wonderful! I still work for the same company. I do miss Tongyeong, though."

"Me too. It feels good to be back."

"*Unnie*, do you want to go out tonight? I'm meeting some old school friends at a restaurant in Gangguan. Kind of like a mini school reunion."

I brightened at the thought of seeing old friends. "Yes. I'd love to come."

"Great. I'll let them know you're coming. They'll be thrilled."

———

In the evening, Seri and I started getting ready to go out. We sat side by side at the makeup table in her bedroom.

"So tell me, is it true that Shin Jinseung and Choi Miyoung are dating?" Seri asked while applying false lashes.

I dropped my lipstick on the floor, startled. *Shin Jinseung and Choi Miyoung?* "Eh? That's the first I've heard of it," I blurted.

"There were rumours flying around while Midnight Dreaming aired that they were a couple in real life."

"I don't know about that. I don't know much about his personal life, but he hasn't mentioned Choi Miyoung at all."

I flashed back to Bora asking, "Who's the better kisser, Chloe or Choi Miyoung?" Based on Jinseung's reply, "It's only acting," it didn't sound as if he had kissed her outside of filming. That was only conjecture, though.

"I hope it's not true…" I murmured.

"Why? Do you like him?"

"No!"

Seri looked at me through narrowed eyes.

"Maybe a little," I admitted.

"*Aigoo*. I'm so jealous. If you do like him, you could actually be in with a chance. You're so beautiful—plus loads of actors fall in love while filming a drama."

"Really?"

"Yeah. It happens all the time."

"Do you remember that he went to Tongyeong High School?"

"Yes. He didn't stand out much back then. If only we'd paid more attention…" She paused in thought before we both cracked up laughing.

When we were ready, we took a taxi to Gangguan Port. The sun melted down over the harbour and lights started switching on, illuminating the area and cascading off the rippling sea in brilliant hues. The fish markets and restaurants bustled with patrons.

We entered a cozy restaurant with a dark wooden interior and enchanting views of the harbour where fishing boats bobbed at their moors.

I spotted a couple of familiar faces at one of the tables. Seri and I approached.

"*Omo*. Chloe Gibson, what brings you back to Tongyeong?" a woman with long brown hair and high cheekbones asked.

"Kim Hana?" I ventured.

She nodded.

"I'm here to visit my host family," I explained.

"And you're in a drama. How cool is that?" a man said. I recognised him but couldn't remember his name.

"What? You're in a drama?" Hana asked, shocked.

I nodded.

"*Aigoo*. Don't you keep up with entertainment news?" the man said. He turned to me. "I'm Do Hanjae, by the way. I was your *seonbae* at Tongyeong High School."

"Is anyone else coming?" Seri asked.

"Bae Yoojin and Hyun Taewoo said they would come. I'm sure they'll be here soon."

"I spread the word on social media, but it seems very few of us are currently in Tongyeong," Hana said.

The remaining guests arrived later, bringing the total to seven of us around the table. Food and drinks included a plentitude of beer and soju, plus seafood dishes and various *banchan*.

We chatted as we ate, talking about our lives since leaving Tongyeong High School. Only a couple of them still lived in Tongyeong, the rest were just visiting like Seri and myself. Everyone seemed the most interested in me, and I spent a large portion of the conversation fielding questions about what it was like to act in a drama.

"My part is not that big," I assured them.

"But you have scenes with Shin Jinseung and Baek Yena, right?" Tae-woo asked.

"Yes. A few. Anyway, enough about me. I want to hear all about what you guys have been up to."

I successfully redirected the conversation away from me, so I could lay back and listen to everyone else's stories.

As the hours passed and the beer and soju flowed, we were starting to get pretty drunk.

"I've got an idea," Hana drunkenly announced.

"What is it?" Seri asked.

She paused for effect. "…Let's go to a *noraebang*!"

"Great idea!"

Others chimed in with approval. We agreed to finish our drinks then head to the karaoke place next door. We were about to get up and leave when a tall man wearing a beanie and a black face mask entered the restaurant and walked over to our table. *Is that…*

"Sorry I'm late," he said.

Shin Jinseung!

"*Omo!*" Hana gasped.

23

J inseung introduced himself to the group. "Hi, I'm Shin Jinseung. I was at Tongyeong High School from 2009 to 2011."

Everyone stared at him, mouths gaping, too starstruck to say anything.

"*Seonbae*," I said. "I thought you weren't coming."

"My scene was cancelled at the last minute, so I could make it after all."

"How did you know to come here?"

"News of this little reunion was all over my social media."

"Oh. Well, sit down."

He took the last empty seat at the table.

"*Seonbae…*" Hana said.

Jinseung turned to her. "Yes?"

"You really came…"

"Of course! I'm a former Tongyeong student, after all."

"We were just about to go to karaoke," I said.

"That sounds good. It will be a little more private too." He looked around nervously at the other patrons.

"Do you want a drink before we go?"

"Nah. It's fine. I'll have something when we get there."

We headed next door to the karaoke place where we booked a large private room. Jinseung ordered and paid for more food and drinks.

The room had black walls and faux leather seats around its perimeter, with a large screen at the end, and a low table in the centre. A mirror ball hung from the ceiling, making specks of light dance around the room.

"Who wants to go first?" Jinseung asked. He turned to me. "Chloe?"

Even though I had drunk a lot, it still didn't feel enough to sing in front of Jinseung.

Seri offered to go first instead. She chose the song "Palette" by IU. It really suited her. She even resembled her a bit.

Jinseung took the stage next, singing "Genie" by Girls' Generation, complete with sexy dance moves. Despite his joking tone, I was pleasantly surprised by his singing voice.

"You could have been an idol," Hana gushed.

I grinned with the secret knowledge of his idol training.

"I could have been in a girl group, right?" Jinseung quipped.

After everyone else had had a turn, I couldn't put it off any longer. I had another shot of soju before grabbing the mic.

Everyone whistled and cheered as I sang, feeding my confidence. I looked Jinseung in the eyes and he grinned back at me, nodding along to the beat of the song.

Several drinks later, we were all singing and dancing together, no concern for how awful we sounded or how stupid our dance moves looked.

Hana had her sights set on Jinseung all night long, and partway through one of the songs, she slipped her arm around him and started to dance with him. Jinseung reciprocated, to Hana's utter delight. I watched on, sick with jealousy. The room spun around me. *I've had waaay too much to drink...*

"Whoa there. You okay?" Jinseung asked. He had broken away from Hana and held out a hand to steady me as I stumbled drunkenly.

"I'm fine," I assured him.

"Doesn't seem like it. Do you want to go outside and get some fresh air?"

"All right. That sounds good."

He told everyone we were heading out for a minute, then donned his face mask and beanie again. I could sense Hana glaring at us as he guided me outside.

We walked across the road to the harbourside, where I leaned against the railing, inhaling the salt air, trying to sober up a bit and stop my head from spinning.

"Feeling better?" Jinseung asked.

"Yeah. I think so."

He stared out at the ocean. "You saved me."

"Huh?"

"You helped me get away from Kim Hana."

"Oh. Did you want to get away from her?" It hadn't seemed as if he weren't enjoying the attention.

"She's a bit full on."

I sighed. "You must get hit on all the time, being a celebrity and all..."

"Yeah. Not that I like it, or anything. Actually, I find it too much."

"I get it."

"Hana didn't take any interest in me in high school, so why now? Because I'm famous. That's all people like her care about."

I didn't take any interest in him in high school either, I thought regretfully.

"Are you cold?" He offered me his jacket.

"No. Not really."

We stood in calm silence, watching the waves crash against the shore.

"Why did you come out tonight?" I asked.

Jinseung smiled. "I might be famous but I'm still an ex-student of Tongyeong High School. Sometimes I want to do ordinary things like go to reunions."

"Ah…I see."

The wind blew my hair in my face. Jinseung held it back, his fingers caressing my face as he did so. He took his beanie off then pulled it onto my head, which kept my hair out of my eyes.

"Cute," he said, grinning.

"Don't you need that?"

He looked around. "There aren't too many people around. It's fine."

The cold ocean wind continued to whip me, drawing a shiver, and I suddenly regretted refusing his jacket. As if reading my mind, he removed his jacket and draped it over my shoulders.

"*Aigoo*. I'm taking all your clothes," I said.

"I don't need them." He gripped the railing, his knuckles pale.

Not thinking what I was doing, I reached out and placed my hand on his. His skin felt cold to the touch. He turned to me, eyebrow raised, and a mildly disapproving look in his eyes. I quickly snatched my hand away, realising I was crossing a line, just like Kim Hana.

"You're cold," I stammered. "We should go back inside."

"I don't want to."

"You can't avoid her all night."

"Oh yes I can. The time in the karaoke room will be up soon, anyway."

I thought they might add some time on, but Jinseung was right. A couple minutes later, the group emerged from the building.

"Chloe!" Seri called out from across the road. "We're leaving now. Are you coming?"

"Uh, yes. Just a minute!" I turned to Jinseung. "I should go with Seri. I'm staying at her parents' place."

"Okay. Maybe I'll catch you around."

"How long are you here for?"

"Until Sunday."

"Okay. Well, I'll still be here. Maybe we'll bump into each other." I returned his jacket and beanie.

"Goodnight. Drink a big glass of water before bed. You need it."

"Thanks for the advice. Goodnight."

Seri stood waiting, arms folded.

"Coming!" I said, crossing the road back to her.

Jinseung stayed by the harbour, looking out at the fishing boats.

"What was that all about?" Seri asked when we were safely inside a taxi on our way home.

"What?"

"You and Shin Jinseung having one-on-one time."

"Oh, he just wanted to get away from Kim Hana."

"Get away from Hana, or be alone with you?"

"Huh? It wasn't like that."

"Are you sure? You were standing so close to each other. And back at karaoke, he couldn't keep his eyes off you."

"Really? Are you sure you're not imagining things?"

"I'm not. Trust me."

I sighed. Even if that were true, he probably gravitated to me simply because he knew me better than everyone else there.

When we arrived back at Seri's house, the lights were off and her parents had already gone to bed. We did our bedtime routines then retired to her room together—the same room we had shared while in high school. Seri used to sleep on the bed, while I slept on the ground on a thin mattress called a *yo*. I actually found it very comfortable, especially since the floor was heated.

Now, the room had been cleared of most of Seri's belongings, and the bed was gone.

"My parents got rid of the bed when I moved out to create more space," Seri explained.

Yos and blankets had already been laid out for us. Her parents must have done so knowing we'd come home tired and drunk.

I slipped beneath the heavy blanket and pulled it up to my chin.

"Goodnight, Chloe," Seri said, before turning off the lamp, engulfing the room in darkness.

With the weight of the quilt on top of me, and my head fuzzy from alcohol, I swiftly fell asleep, deep and dreamless.

I didn't wake up until morning light seeped through the gaps in the curtains. The sunlight stung my pupils when I opened my eyes, causing me to clench them shut again. My head felt like it was going to explode, and my mouth and throat were like sandpaper. I let out a deep groan.

When I could finally open my eyes, I rolled over to see if Seri was still in bed. Her *yo* was empty, the quilt pulled down in a wrinkled pile at its foot. *She must have gotten up already.*

Gathering all my strength, I peeled myself out of bed and marched directly to the kitchen to get a glass of water. A hearty, beef-flavoured smell wafted in the air growing stronger as I approached. The source of the fumes became apparent when I saw Mrs. Soo boiling a pot on the stove.

"That smells wonderful. What is it?" I asked.

"Hangover soup," she replied.

"That's exactly what I need."

"I thought so. It'll be ready in a few minutes."

I poured myself a glass of water, then walked over to the table. Seri sat there, texting someone on her phone. She looked up when she noticed me approach. "Oh, you're up," she said. "I was just about to go and get you. How are you feeling?"

"I've been better," I admitted. I sat down and chugged the tall glass of water, relieving my dry mouth.

Mrs. Soo served us the steaming soup, ladling it into large bowls.

"*Eomma* makes the best hangover soup," Seri said. "You'll feel better in no time."

After two bowls of delicious soup, it was as if my internal battery had been recharged. I was ready to face the day.

"It worked!" I exclaimed.

"Told ya," Seri said.

Snow came up to me, sniffing around my feet. I gave her a pat and she wagged her tail, panting.

"Would you like to go for a walk, Snow?" I rubbed her furry tummy.

Snow let out a delighted bark.

"Can I take Snow for a walk?" I asked Mrs. Soo.

"Oh, would you? That would be great. She'll love it."

"Okay. A walk will help clear my head too. Where's her lead?"

Mrs. Soo retrieved the lead which made Snow jump up and down with excitement.

"Settle down, Snow," Mrs. Soo said, as she attached it to her collar.

"All right. I'm going now," I said.

"When you come back, do you want to go to the *jjimjilb-bang* with me?" Seri asked.

"Sure. I shouldn't be too long."

I set out with Snow. She ran so fast ahead that it was like she was walking me, not the other way around. Eventually she settled into an easier pace. The fresh sea breeze woke up my senses as we followed a walking trail around the coastline. Sunlight gleamed off the gentle ocean waves. *Ahhhh…this is the life. Maybe I should try to get a teaching job in Tongyeong once I'm through with the drama?*

While I ambled along, lost in thought, Snow started whining and going crazy. She pulled at the lead and I lost my grip. I was powerless to stop her as she bounded into the distance, disappearing from my line of vision.

24

"Snow!" I called after the runaway dog. "Snoooow!"

I ran and ran until I finally caught sight of her. She was playing with another dog—a cute little Maltese.

"There you are!" I said, relieved.

A voice came from nearby. "Looks like we had the same idea."

I shot up, startled. It was Shin Jinseung's lovely deep voice. He stood watching me, an amused expression on his face.

"*Seonbae*, is that your dog?" I asked.

"His name's Buster," Jinseung said.

"He's adorable." I picked up the fluffy white dog and cuddled him. He licked my arm with his tiny pink tongue.

"He likes you." He petted Snow. "Good boy."

"It's a girl. Her name's Snow. She belongs to my host family."

"Good girl, Snow."

I let Buster down and he immediately went back to playing with Snow.

"They get along," Jinseung said. "Shall we walk them together?"

"Okay."

We walked along the quiet trail, side by side, bathed in morning sunlight.

"It's a beautiful morning." I inhaled a deep breath of fresh air.

"Do you have a hangover?"

"Yes, but I'm getting over it. What about you?"

"No. I don't think I drank as much as you since I arrived late."

The dogs kept criss-crossing around each other causing their leads to tangle.

"*Aigoo*." Jinseung got down on his knees and unwound them.

We had arrived in a picturesque park area overlooking the sea, so we slowed down to take in the views.

"Could you take a photo of me and Buster?" Jinseung asked. "I want something to post to social media."

"Sure."

He passed me his phone, then posed holding Buster.

I took several photos while gushing about how cute they looked. "Your fans will love this," I said.

As I reviewed the photos, I noticed something in his gallery. The video of our practice kiss. "Huh? I thought you were going to delete that video."

"What? Oh that." Jinseung's face reddened. "I forgot about it. I should delete it." He grabbed his phone and did so, right in front of me.

My heart sank as I watched the file disappear. I wished I had a copy. I'd play it over and over again. That kiss, although pretend, had been so amazing, it made my knees weak just thinking about it. The way he held me up close, the softness of his lips…

"You okay?" Jinseung asked.

"Oh? Yes. Sorry. I zoned out for a second there."

We carried on walking, passing by a café on the marina surrounded by outdoor seating bustling with people enjoying a morning coffee.

"Jinseungie!" a female voice called.

Uh oh. Someone has recognised him.

Jinseung stopped in his tracks and watched the woman wave to him.

"*Eomma*," Jinseung said under his breath.

"That's your mother?" I asked.

"Yes. I should go say hi."

I went with him to his mother, a glamorous-looking woman with short hair, wearing a dress and a pearl necklace. She sat opposite another, similarly glamorous woman.

"*Eomma*. Don't call out my name like that in public," Jinseung said.

"Oh, I'm sorry." Her eyes switched to me. "*Omo*. Who's this? Can it be? Does my Jinseungie have a girlfriend?"

I dropped Snow's lead in shock at the word "girlfriend."

"This is Chloe Gibson, *Eomma*. My co-star in Hidden History. I told you about her, remember?"

"Didn't you go to Tongyeong High School?" the other woman asked.

"That's right," I replied.

"I think you were in the same year as my daughter, Gu Eunjae."

"Yes. I remember her. She was in my class."

"So you went to Tongyeong High School? I thought you looked familiar," Jinseung's mother said, her eyes still narrowed in suspicion. "Are you sure you're not dating? I'm quite modern, you know. I wouldn't mind a non-Korean daughter-in-law."

"*Eomma!* Leave her alone," Jinseung said.

"We're not dating," I said, shuffling my feet in embarrassment.

Her eyes continued to scan me up and down. "Dating or not, you two seem very close. Chloe Gibson, why don't you come over for dinner tonight? I'd love to have you over."

I gaped at her suggestion, unable to respond.

"We already have dinner plans," Jinseung said quickly.

My eyes widened in surprise. Jinseung threw me a look which said to play along.

"*Omo.*" Jinseung's mother clutched a hand to her chest. "Dinner plans? Alone together? And you say you're not dating."

"We're friends," Jinseung said. "Can't two friends eat alone together?"

"Can you be friends with such an attractive girl?"

"*Eomma!*"

"Okay, well, whatever you say. Have fun tonight."

I gave the pair of women a bow before Jinseung led me away.

"Sorry about that," he said once safely out of earshot of the women. "My mum can be a bit extreme. I've never introduced her to a girl before. She's always asking when I'll bring someone home to meet her and my dad."

"What did you mean by dinner plans?" I asked. "Did you say that just to get me out of having dinner with your parents?"

Jinseung shook his head. "Actually, I was planning on asking you to have dinner with me anyway."

"Really?" I raised a sceptical brow.

"Not as a date or anything!" he quickly added. "I mean, you know how I went to the reunion last night?"

"Yeah…"

"Well, I liked going out and feeling like a normal person for once. It feels that way when I'm in Tongyeong. I don't get to experience it often."

"I…kind of get that."

"So what do you say? Will you go out with me tonight?"

I mulled his proposal over. There was just one detail which made me hesitate. "I know you say it's not a date, but won't it look like that? What if it fuels dating rumours?"

"I know the owner of the restaurant. He'll make sure we're seated privately and that no one bothers us. And besides, it's not a date. We're friends and colleagues. Why shouldn't we have dinner together?"

"I guess I'm overthinking things."

Jinseung gave my shoulder a little squeeze. "I appreciate your concern."

The two dogs yapped at another passing dog. I held tightly onto Snow's lead, worried that she might escape again. My arms were starting to tire from holding her back.

"I better get going," I said eventually. "I've already stayed out far longer than I intended."

"I'll walk you back," Jinseung said.

We turned to follow the trail back in the other direction. He walked me all the way to my host family's house.

"So this is where you lived," he said, surveying the property from the bottom of the driveway.

"Yup."

"We lived so close to each other. It's crazy how things turned out."

Snow whined, sticking to Buster's side longingly.

"The dogs don't want to part," I said.

"Sorry, Buster. We have to go now." He tugged him away. "See you tonight, Chloe. I'll pick you up, say, around seven-thirty?"

I nodded.

"I'll see you then. Come on, Buster."

———

"You're going out for dinner with Shin Jinseung?!" Seri said loudly while we sat together, naked, in a public bath.

"Shhhh…keep it down," I said.

"*Omo*. Sorry."

I looked around, making sure the other bathers weren't paying us any attention before I replied. "Yes. I'm going tonight."

"Wow. Is it a date?"

"No. It's just as friends."

"Oh really?"

"Yes. Really."

Seri pouted. "That's too bad."

"Jinseung's mother seemed convinced we were dating too. I met her while we were out walking."

"His mum? Shin Jinseung's ideal type is someone who gets along with his family, you know."

"Is it? How do you know that?"

"That's what the internet says. I think he said that in an interview one time."

"They always answer something like that. 'Someone who gets along with my family', 'someone who's mature and respectful.' Do you think they'd say 'someone who has a sexy body'?"

"So cynical. Anyway, you do have a sexy body."

I folded my arms to cover my boobs. "*Aigoo*. I shouldn't go bathing with a pervert."

She ignored my comment. "When we get home, let me help you get ready. I want to live this night vicariously through you. Text me updates throughout the night."

"No."

"Please? Not even a couple of short messages?"

"…Maybe."

"Yes!" She pumped her fist.

———

Jinseung's crisp, freshly ironed white shirt and the upscale restaurant we arrived at made me question if it really were a date, because it felt suspiciously like one.

Suddenly I wished I'd put more effort into my appearance, feeling self-conscious in jeans, when a skirt or dress would have been more appropriate. A bit more makeup also wouldn't have hurt.

The owner of the restaurant greeted Jinseung as an old friend and directed us to a privately located table. Large windows presented a view of the sky, scattered with thousands of twinkling stars, and the Tongyeong landscape: buildings with illuminated windows and signs surrounding the placid harbour, lush green hills, and dark islands in the distance.

I looked out, absorbing the beautiful sight. "It's stunning…"

"It's a nice spot, isn't it?" Jinseung said, standing next to me.

"Makes me feel like I want to live here again."

"In Tongyeong?"

I nodded. "Maybe I could look for a teaching job—"

"Why don't you stay in Seoul?" Jinseung interjected.

I shrugged. "I will if I can make it work."

"This is a nice place, but it does get boring."

"Well, that's true I suppose…"

"You should stay in Seoul."

"You think so?"

"I do."

"Hmmm…" I continued looking out the window, deep in thought. *Should I really stay in Seoul?* I had come here to experience the vibrant city I had witnessed in countless K-dramas, but since my arrival I'd felt continually on edge and way out of my comfort zone. I sighed, ruminating on the fact that my life would be one big question mark after Hidden History wrapped.

"Take a seat," Jinseung urged, tearing me from my thoughts.

He pulled out a chair for me, and I sat down, peeling my eyes away from the view to open a menu.

"You like steak, right?" he said. "It's great here."

"I'm in Tongyeong. I should get seafood."

"Get whatever you like, and as your *seonbae*, I'm paying."

"You don't have to—"

He raised his hand. "Not another word. I insist."

I sheepishly returned to examining the menu.

After an inordinate amount of time deciding, we finally placed our orders.

The waiter brought out the wine first and poured us each a glass.

"Hey, Chloe," Jinseung said after downing a generous sip.

"Mmm?"

"We're friends, right?"

"Yes. Of course."

Jinseung rubbed the stem of the wine glass between his fingers. "I don't mind if you use *banmal* with me outside of work."

My mouthful of wine went down the wrong way and I coughed. *Banmal? He's asking me to get closer with him…*

"You okay?" Jinseung asked.

"Yes," I said, regaining my composure. "So…You want me to speak casually with you. I think I can do that."

"And why don't you drop the *seonbae?*"

"What should I call you then? Jinseung-ssi?"

He shook his head. "Too polite."

"Jinseung-ah?…*Oppa*?"

The left corner of his mouth lifted into a charming lopsided smile. "I like *Oppa*. Call me *Oppa*."

My cheeks flushed with warmth. "Okay, *Oppa*."

"I like it, *Dongseang*."

A giggle escaped my mouth.

"What's so funny?" he asked, amused.

"I don't think anyone's called me a *dongseang* before."

"You look cute when you laugh."

"You say that a lot."

"What?"

"Cute," I said, mimicking the deadpan way he said it.

"I don't sound like that."

"Yes you do."

"No, I don't." He lightly kicked me under the table.

"Hey!"

He did it again.

"Cut it out!"

We didn't notice the waiter approach with our meals until he placed them on the table, interrupting our flirty exchange. We bashfully reverted to acting like adults.

A grilled mackerel lay on the large white plate in front of me, skin lightly salted and charred to form a golden-brown crust.

I picked up a piece with my chopsticks and deposited it into my mouth, where it practically melted on my tongue.

"How is it?" Jinseung asked.

"Delicious!" I exclaimed.

We ate in silence, revelling in the delectable flavour of the fish until Jinseung stopped suddenly, a thought appearing to strike him as he toyed with his chopsticks. "Chloe, can I ask you something?"

"Sure, what is it?"

"Why did you come back to Korea?"

I paused, wondering how much to tell him. "To escape," I said eventually.

"What is it that you wanted to escape?"

"Various things…"

"What exactly?"

"It's a long story."

"I'm happy to listen."

"Well, all right then. If you insist."

Jinseung leaned in ready to listen attentively.

I took a moment to get the story straight in my head before starting. "Just a couple years ago I had everything going for me," I began. "I was fresh out of university with a business degree. I had an amazing boyfriend, and a job offer from a cool new startup company, but within a few months everything fell apart. The job wasn't the dream job I thought it would be. I was a 'customer experience specialist'—a fancy name for customer service rep. I quickly realised the company was short-staffed. Customer calls and emails piled up at a rate faster than my team could answer them. This meant working nights, weekends, public holidays…sometimes weeks would pass without having a day off. We weren't paid overtime."

"That's horrible."

"That's not all. Our boss micromanaged us, and if anyone made a mistake they would be singled out and shamed in front of the whole company. It happened to me several times. The pressure was relentless. To top it all off, I learned from a friend that my boyfriend was cheating on me. While I worked late, he was meeting up with another girl. We had a huge argument and split up. I had to move out of the flat we shared and into a grotty house with five flatmates and one bathroom."

"Did you quit the job?"

I nodded. "I ended up fainting at work one day. I was hospitalised. The diagnosis—too much stress. I decided then and there that I wouldn't return to work. I quit the job, left my flatmates, and moved back in with my parents."

"Sounds like that was for the best."

"Yeah, but after my experience at the startup, I developed an anxiety around working, which stopped me from applying to new jobs. Instead, I stayed at home all day lazing around watching K-dramas. "

"You deserved some time to relax and recover."

"That's what I kept telling myself. My parents were supportive at first too, but as the months passed, it was no secret that they were growing frustrated by my reluctance to work or to contribute to the household in any way. They told me that I would have to start paying rent if I wanted to stay at home, and that would mean getting a job."

"An ultimatum."

"Exactly, and I hated them for it. Fortunately, it wasn't long before I had an epiphany, and it came from watching K-dramas of all things."

"The decision to teach English in Korea?"

"Right. I had always wanted to go back anyway."

"I see. So that's how it happened. Chloe…"

"Hmmm?"

"You've revealed a lot to me. Now I feel like I have to come clean about something."

25

W*hat is it? What is he going to say?* My mind reeled with possibilities.

Just as Jinseung was about to open his mouth to speak, a shrill voice pierced our bubble.

"Jinseungie! Chloe!"

Jinseung gritted his teeth in annoyance.

His mother, and a man I assumed to be his father, now occupied the only table visible from ours. She walked over to us.

"What a pleasant surprise," she said.

"Why are you here?" Jinseung asked, irritated.

"Since you weren't home for dinner, we decided to go out to eat as well."

"To the same restaurant?"

"You never told us what restaurant you were going to. It's just a coincidence we're all here. Maybe I should ask if we can join our tables together?"

"There's no need. We're nearly finished eating and we'll be leaving soon."

"*Yeobo*, leave them be," Jinseung's father said.

"This is the girl I was telling you about," Jinseung's mother explained to him. "They look good together, don't you think?"

"*Eomma!*" Jinseung said.

"Okay, okay. I won't bother you anymore. Finish your meal." She retreated to her table in a huff.

"Sorry about that," Jinseung said, returning his attention to me.

He ate another piece of fish, appearing to forget what we were talking about before the interruption.

I couldn't let it pass. I needed to know what he had to come clean about.

"What were you going to tell me?" I asked.

Jinseung swallowed his mouthful. "I can't say it with my parents right there, spying on us."

I sighed. "Fair enough. Tell me later, when we're alone."

He nodded and continued to eat.

I played with my food, suddenly losing my appetite.

"Are you finished?" Jinseung asked when he had emptied his plate.

"Yes. It was a bit too much for me."

We polished off the rest of the wine before getting up to leave. I gave his parents a quick bow as Jinseung tugged me to the counter. He tried to pay the bill, but they said his parents had already paid. Jinseung heaved a sigh.

"They didn't have to do that," he murmured.

The cool night air hit us as we exited the restaurant. Jinseung put his hoodie on and pulled the hood over his head.

"Come on," he said. "I'll walk you home."

He cast a cautious glance around before we set out, walking side by side down a quiet route through residential streets, dimly lit by streetlights and the glowing full moon.

"Sorry about my mother," Jinseung said. "She has a habit of trying to get involved in my relationships."

"I don't mind. Anyway, I'm sure she didn't intend to crash our evening."

He scoffed. "I'm sure she did."

My thoughts drifted back in the direction of our conversation over dinner. Now was my chance to bring it up again. "*Oppa*…"

"Yes?"

"What were you going to tell me before?"

Jinseung paused and rubbed the side of his broad neck. "About that…I've changed my mind."

I froze in my tracks, stunned. "What?"

"I don't want to tell you because it might put ideas in your head."

"But now that you've mentioned it, you have to tell me."

"Is that a rule?"

"Yes."

"I don't think it is."

"You're seriously not going to tell me?"

"Hmmm…Not right now."

"This is going to drive me crazy, you know that?"

"*Aigoo*." A smile crept onto his lips. "Then how about this? Let's play a little game."

My interest was piqued. "Game?"

"If I win, I get to keep my secret. If you win, I'll tell you everything."

He's loving this. He has me right under his thumb. I pursed my lips in frustration.

"What? You don't want to play?" he teased.

I crossed my arms. "Fine! Whatever you want. Let's do it."

"Okay…First person to run to that tree over there, wins." He pointed to a large tree in the distance.

"No fair! You're faster than me."

"I'll give you a three-second head start."

"Hmmm…" *Will that be enough?*

"You in?" he asked.

"All right. Let's go."

"On the count of three. One…two…three…go!"

I sped off towards the lone, tall tree across a field of grass. I didn't look over my shoulder to see how far Jinseung was behind me, but I could hear his breath when he had just about caught up. The tree was just a few metres away.

So…close…

Jinseung grabbed me by the waist and flung me backwards. *Oh no you don't!* I caught the back of his hoodie and pulled him with me. I didn't let go even when I lost my footing. I fell down on my butt, and Jinseung came tumbling down on top of me, our legs interlaced, his panting body covering mine.

His right hand landed on the ground. His left hand was on my chest. I froze, unable to process the compromising position we had ended up in.

Jinseung's intense, charismatic eyes locked onto mine and he swallowed hard. We stayed fixed in that position until he suddenly realised where his left hand was.

"*Omo!*" he snatched it back, then hurriedly detangled himself from me and got up.

Back on his two feet, he reached out, held my hands, and pulled me up. "Sorry," he stammered. "I didn't mean to do that."

"I know. It's okay."

"Are you hurt?"

"No. I don't think so. You?"

"I'm fine."

We brushed blades of grass off our clothes.

"No one won. What do we do now?" I asked.

"You didn't win, so I'm not telling you."

I eyed the tree. *Who said the game was over?*

Jinseung noticed what I was looking at, but it was too late to stop me.

I jumped over and touched the tree. "I win."

"*Aigoo*. You want to know that badly, huh?"

"Yes!"

"Okay. Here goes…" He suddenly turned shy, colour rising in his cheeks. "…I had a huge crush on you in high school."

"Huh?"

"There. It's out in the open."

26

I could feel my cheeks turn red. *Jinseung liked me in high school? I can't believe it…*

"Say something," Jinseung urged.

"I'm shocked," I spluttered.

"Is it really that surprising? Lots of guys liked you. I pretended not to care, but in reality, I was no better than them, fawning over a girl because she looked different. I've grown up a lot since then, of course. "

I turned this new piece of information over in my mind, unsure what to make of it. "Why didn't you want to tell me?" I asked at last.

"I didn't want you to get the wrong idea. I liked you in high school, but it's not like I'm gonna date you now just 'cause of something like that. I'm completely over it."

The snark in his voice made my blood pressure rise. "I wasn't thinking that," I bit back.

"Good."

An awkward silence lingered over us as we walked the rest

of the way to the house. Try as I might, I couldn't hide my annoyance at Jinseung's comment.

"Are you angry with me?" he asked when we reached the bottom of the driveway.

"No," I said, my tone bitter.

"It seems like you are."

"I'm not."

"Well, okay…" He didn't sound convinced.

"Thanks for dinner."

"That's all right."

"Goodnight."

"Goodnight." He turned away and disappeared into the shadowy night, not glancing back even once. I slipped inside the house with a sigh.

"*Unnie*," came Seri's voice out of nowhere, startling me.

She appeared in the hallway, wrapped in a fuzzy pink dressing gown, her hair held back by a cat-ear hairband.

"Why do you have dirt all over you?" she asked, brow furrowed.

"I, uh, fell on the ground."

"*Aigoo*. So clumsy."

"Yeah."

"So…how did it go?"

"I don't know. Good and bad."

"Hmm? Come here and tell me what happened." She ushered me into her bedroom.

I explained what had happened as I changed into my pyjamas and did my nighttime skincare routine.

"I was beginning to let myself believe that he might actually like me," I admitted, as we lay on the *yos*, moisturising sheet masks adhered to our faces. "Then he comes out and says something like that. *It's not like I'm gonna date you now,*" I imitated his tone.

"Hmmm…" Seri fiddled with the edge of the blanket. "Could it be that he does like you, but he doesn't know if it will be possible to date you?"

"What do you mean?"

"Well, dating is so hard for celebrities. There's a lot he would have to take into consideration. It would no doubt harm his career, not to mention the hordes of jealous fans that could go after you."

I sighed, knowing she talked sense. "I suppose so. But still…"

"Don't jump to any conclusions. That's my advice."

We removed our sheet masks and tucked ourselves back into bed.

With the lights off, my mind raced, analysing the night's events over and over. Could Seri be right? Maybe he does want to date me, he just…*can't*. Either way, it was frustrating.

My phone screen lit up with an incoming message, distracting me from my thoughts.

Bora: Breaking news. The air date of Hidden History has been brought forward two weeks. Not much time to go now! PS. Check the mail tomorrow. I sent you a package.

Chloe: What package?

Bora: You'll see. Goodnight!

27

The powerful stench of raw fish filled my nostrils making my stomach churn. I tried to breathe through my mouth instead as I walked around the fish market with Seri and Mrs. Soo.

"This is just like old times," Mrs. Soo said, linking arms with us. "You two used to come with me to the fish market every week."

"I've missed it," I said. "But I haven't missed the smell."

"What are you talking about? There's nothing better than the smell of fresh fish." She breathed in a great whiff of air. "Ahhhh!"

Seri and I exchanged amused looks and giggled.

All around us, *ajummas* wearing sun visors and rubber gloves crouched over colourful buckets of squirming and flopping live fish.

Mrs. Soo stopped at a stall selling shellfish and bartered with the vendor for a large box of oysters.

After purchasing the oysters, a nearby sweet stall caught

her eye. "Let's have a treat," she said. "You girls used to love eating *kkoolbbang*."

She bought three *kkoolbbang*—balls of sweet red bean paste, encased in deep fried dough and smothered in sticky honey syrup, topped off with a light sprinkling of sesame seeds.

I took one small bite and its sugary sweetness exploded in my mouth. I ate slowly, savouring the rest of the *kkoolbbang* as we walked back to the house.

Upon returning home, Mrs. Soo stumbled over a package on the doorstep. She bent down and examined the label. "It's for you, Chloe."

"Oooh…What's that?" Seri asked.

"I'm not sure," I replied, picking up the package.

I could feel a thick document within the padded courier bag and understanding dawned on me.

I grabbed a pair of scissors from the kitchen and opened it up. Sure enough, it was a Hidden History script. Episode 10.

Bora had attached a fluorescent-pink post-it note to the front with some page numbers scrawled on it. I flicked to the pages she had noted—flashback scenes involving my character.

I had already filmed several flashbacks in advance, but these were new scenes. I'd need to go back to Seoul soon, I realised. I could be called on set at any time. My stay in Tongyeong would have to come to an end sooner than I anticipated.

"What is it?" Seri asked, leaning over my shoulder.

I cradled the script to my chest. "It's confidential."

"Let me see!"

I loosened my grip. "Okay. I'm not really supposed to share this, so you have to promise to keep it secret."

"I promise."

I passed the script to her outstretched hands.

She flipped through its pages, intrigued. "So this is what a drama script looks like…Need any help practicing your lines?"

"Yeah, if you're offering."

"Let's do it."

We sat down together and read through the scenes featuring my character. Seri gave it her best effort, altering her voice and actions for each character she portrayed.

"You're much better at this than Yang Bora," I commented.

"Who's she?"

"An intern at KAM. She's kind of like my manager now."

"Oh, I see."

After several run-throughs, Mrs. Soo brought in a tray of freshly made rolls of *gimbap.* "Have something to eat," she urged. "You can't work well on an empty stomach."

"Thanks, *Eomma*," Seri said.

"Thank you," I echoed, helping myself to one of the rolls.

We were about to get back to work when my phone buzzed. My heart skipped a beat at Jinseung's name. I opened the message.

Jinseung: Want a ride back to Seoul tomorrow?

I started to type a reply then promptly deleted it.

"Who are you texting?" Seri asked.

"No one." I shielded my phone screen from her.

"It's Shin Jinseung, isn't it? Gimme." She grabbed my phone and read the message. "Are you going to go?" she asked.

"I haven't decided yet."

"Won't you need to film these scenes soon? You'll need to go back to Seoul."

"Yes, but I was hoping to spend a few more days here first." I stroked my chin in thought. "Then again, it would be very convenient to have a ride home…"

"And a convenient excuse to be alone with Shin Jinseung."

I rolled my eyes. "I'm still mad at him, remember?"

"Just go with him. I know you want to."

"Are you that desperate to get rid of me?"

"You know I'm not. But let's face it, there's not much to do here. It's too boring to stay for more than a few days. Besides, I'll definitely be heading to Seoul soon as well. We'll see each other again."

I sighed. "I guess you're right. Then should I just tell him I'll go with him?"

"Of course."

I can't stay mad at him forever, I decided. I replied to his message, agreeing to the ride.

Jinseung replied almost instantly:

Jinseung: I'll pick you up tomorrow afternoon

─────

The next morning, I walked Snow along the coastline one last time. I took my time absorbing the sights and sounds, as if trying to imprint the city in my mind. *Goodbye, Tongyeong. I hope to see you again soon.*

When I got back to the house, I started to pack my things. I hadn't brought much with me, so it didn't take long.

I ate lunch with my host family, then we said our goodbyes.

"If things don't work out in Seoul, you're always welcome here, and you can stay as long as you need to," Mrs. Soo said.

"Thanks. I appreciate that," I said.

Right on cue, Jinseung's car rumbled up the driveway.

"He's here," I said, looking out the window.

"Have a nice drive back," Mr. Han said.

I hugged the family members one more time before leaving.

Jinseung came out of the car, wearing a white t-shirt, blue jeans, and a cap on his head.

"Are you ready?" he asked.

"Yes," I replied.

"Let's go."

He took my bag from me and hurled it into the boot of his black SUV.

I said few words as I got seated in the car, Jinseung's comment from the other day still heavy on my mind.

"Are you still mad at me?" Jinseung asked, picking up on my icy demeanour.

I shook my head.

"So you admit you *were* mad at me."

"I wasn't—" I sighed, unwilling to start an argument. "I'm sorry."

"It's okay."

"Thanks for offering me a ride back."

"No problem. We're going to the same place anyway. It would have been rude not to offer." He reached his arm behind my seat and turned his head to look out the rear window as he reversed. I bit my lip, admiring the tantalising curvature of his bicep until he snapped away to put the car into drive.

"Let's put some music on. What do you like to listen to?" he asked.

"K-pop," I answered. "Astro, Got7, B1A4."

He sighed. "Not that."

"BtoB? ShiNEE?"

"I'll put something else on." He scrolled through the tracks on the LCD screen on the dashboard.

I crossed my arms. "Why even bother asking my opinion?"

"I thought you might have good taste in music," he chided. "Ah, let's listen to this." He turned the volume dial up and Korean rap music started to blast out.

"Agghh! My ears." I covered them in mock horror.

"Would you rather sit in silence?"

"Yes."

"Okay. That's all right with me. Silence it is." He turned the music off, much to my relief.

Before long, we were out of Tongyeong and cruising along the highway. I felt comfortable in the car with Jinseung driving. He handled his car with ease, steering smoothly and paying attention to the road.

"You're a good driver," I commented.

"*Aigoo*. You know how to stroke a man's ego. To be honest, I'm used to Changsoo *Hyung* driving me everywhere. I rarely go on outings by myself—or with a passenger. It's nice to go for a drive. I've missed it."

"Sorry I made you turn the music off before…You can put it back on again if you like."

"It's okay. It gives me a headache after a while anyway."

Partway through the journey, I let out a large yawn.

"Are you tired?" Jinseung asked.

"Long car rides always make me feel drowsy."

"You can have a nap if you want."

I snorted at the idea, but eventually I let my head flop against the window, and the rhythmic vibrations of the car began to lull me. *Maybe a nap isn't such a bad idea.* I reached under the seat, wondering how to recline it.

"What are you doing?" Jinseung asked.

"How do I recline the seat?"

"Going to have a nap after all?"

"Yes."

"There's a lever at the side."

"Ah. Found it." I adjusted the seat into a comfy position, lay my head down, and soon enough I drifted off.

Bizarre dreams played in my head, punctuated by moments of waking in confusion whenever the car hit a bump.

The next time I woke up, the car had stopped. Jinseung hovered over me, so close I could feel his breath on my cheek.

"Am I still dreaming?" I asked.

"No," he replied.

"What are you doing?"

"Wiping your drool off the seat."

"I don't drool!"

"Oh yes you do!" He dabbed at the seat and my mouth with a tissue. "There."

"I didn't drool," I said again, pouting.

"I have photographic evidence, you know."

I gasped. "You didn't!"

"Look." He thrust his phone in front of me, a photo of my sleeping form on the screen. I had a stupid look on my face, and yes, a tiny bit of dribble trailed from the corner of my mouth.

"Delete that!"

Jinseung snatched the phone away from me. "No. It's cute. Should I make it my screensaver?"

"Don't!"

"Then I'll make it your photo on your contact." He tapped away on his screen. "Done."

"You're so mean."

"I'll delete it if you let me take another photo of you…"

"Forget it."

"Come on."

I sighed, exasperated. "All right then. But you have to let me check if it looks good."

"Okay." He aimed his lens at me, and I posed with a V sign next to my face.

"Gimme," I said, after he had taken the photo.

He passed me his phone and I checked the image. "That's better. You can keep that one and delete that sleeping one."

He did so, and made the other picture my contact photo, a pleased grin on his face.

For the first time since waking up, I looked around, taking in our surroundings. We appeared to be in an underground carpark.

"Where are we?" I asked.

"In the carpark of my apartment building," Jinseung said.

"We're here already? You didn't take me home."

"I don't pay much attention when Bong Changsoo is driving, so I don't know the exact address of your place. I didn't want to wake you up to ask. You looked so peaceful."

"Oh, I see. Well, I'm awake now, so will you be able to drop me at my place?" My stomach growled with hunger and I clutched it in embarrassment. "On second thought, do you happen to have any food in your apartment? I'm starving."

"Even if I did, I can't let you in my apartment."

"Why not?"

"I never take girls up to my apartment."

"Never?"

"Well, I try not to make a habit of it. The other residents will gossip, and I don't want to get a reputation."

I sighed dramatically. "Fine. Just take me home then."

Jinseung started the car and drove to the carpark exit. The gate slowly rolled open. It poured with rain outside.

"Huh? What's going on here?" Jinseung asked.

A truck blocked the street. Jinseung honked his horn, but then realised there was no driver in the truck.

"Fantastic," he said. "We're stuck."

28

"Under no circumstances will I let you stay the night in my apartment," Jinseung said. "Understood?"

"Under—wait, what?" I paused, confused. "Who said anything about staying the night? I wasn't even thinking about that."

"Uh…Just trying to cover my bases. You can come in and have something to eat. That's it. And if the truck still hasn't moved after that, you can take a taxi home."

"Okay."

I followed Jinseung to the elevator, where he swiped a key card and punched the button for the 20th floor. Standing side by side, alone together in tight proximity made my skin prickle and my heart speed up. *He's actually taking me up to his apartment. Reluctantly, but still…*

The elevator stopped at the ground floor. Jinseung instantly pulled away from me before the door opened.

A man entered and pushed the button for the sixth floor. He didn't so much as glance at us, but Jinseung didn't speak or look at me while he was there.

When the man exited, Jinseung visibly relaxed, his posture drooping.

"Pretending not to know me?" I asked.

"I have to be careful," he explained.

We arrived at the 20th floor. Jinseung led me to his apartment door, entered the code, and let me inside.

I took off my shoes and looked around. The apartment was large, but by no means extravagant. A small entranceway led through to an open-plan lounge, kitchen, and dining area decked out with high-end furniture and appliances.

Framed art and photographs hung on the walls, and house plants added a splash of greenery to the decor. Floor-to-ceiling windows provided an expansive view of metropolitan Seoul.

"Nice place," I said, wandering around and taking everything in.

"Thanks," Jinseung said.

I peeked through an open door into another room where a king-size bed dominated the floorspace, and dark walls gave a masculine vibe.

"That's my bedroom," Jinseung said from behind me with an unamused tone.

"*Omo!* Sorry. I was being nosy." I averted my gaze from the room and followed him to the kitchen.

I sat down on a bar stool at the bench while he inspected the fridge and cupboards, which appeared to be empty.

"*Aigoo…*" Jinseung said, scratching his head.

Eventually he located a lone packet of *ramyeon*.

"Is this all right?" he asked.

"Yes. I like *ramyeon*."

"I would have cooked you something proper, but I don't have any ingredients."

"You can cook?"

"Well, more or less. What about you?"

"Yes, I can. I don't know how to cook Korean food, though."

"What can you cook?"

"I can cook a roast meal."

"Ah, very British. I'd like to try that some time."

"I can make it for you if you like."

Jinseung smirked. "I might take you up on that one time."

He put a pot on the stove. While waiting for the water to boil he grabbed a beer from the fridge.

"Would you like something to drink?" he asked.

"Yes please. I'll have a beer too, if there's another one."

He opened two bottles of beer and passed one to me. I took a swig and let out a groan of satisfaction. I probably got dehydrated during the car trip. I gulped down more of the drink.

"Take it easy," Jinseung teased.

Right on cue, I launched into a coughing fit. Jinseung spun me around and patted my back until I stopped.

"Glass of water?" he offered.

"Yes please," I rasped.

The glass of water calmed my angry throat, but then my stomach started making rumbling noises from hunger. I blushed with embarrassment.

"The *ramyeon* won't take long to cook," Jinseung said.

"*Aigoo.*"

"You're cute when you make that face."

"There it is again."

"What?"

"Cute," I mimicked.

"Can't I say that?"

"I can't tell whether you mean it or if you're making fun of me."

"It's a bit of both," Jinseung said, grinning.

I scrunched up my face in frustration.

"That's not so cute," he chided.

"Whatever." I stuck my tongue out at him.

Jinseung added the dry cake of noodles into the boiling water, then rummaged in the fridge again.

"I wonder if these are still okay?" He sniffed at a bunch of green onions and an open packet of mushrooms. "I think they're fine…"

He chopped them up and added them to the pot along with a couple of eggs.

He brought the steaming pot to the table, then ladled the noodles and bright red broth into large bowls. My mouth watered. I grabbed my chopsticks and ate with fierce hunger.

Jinseung watched me in amusement. "You look like you're enjoying that."

"It's good," I said, mouth half full.

"I'm glad."

When I finished eating, it hit me that Jinseung would make me leave soon. The rain continued to pour—even more heavily now. I wished I could stay longer—at least until the rain let up.

Jinseung ate his noodles slowly.

"It's still raining…" I said, head tilted towards the window.

"Yes. It is."

I sighed. "I guess I should order a taxi now."

He didn't say anything or even react.

It seems he really does want me to leave now. I retrieved my phone from my pocket and pulled up the taxi app. "What's the address of this building?"

"It's…" Jinseung put his chopsticks down. "Wait."

"Hmmm?"

"Since you're here now, do you want to hang out a bit

longer? I mean, it doesn't really make a difference whether you leave now or in a couple of hours."

"Well, if it's okay with you…"

"It's okay."

"As long as I don't stay the night?"

"Right." He coughed slightly.

I couldn't contain my smile. *He wants me to stay after all.*

"I'll take these." I cleared our bowls and the pot, taking them to the kitchen. Jinseung followed me to help.

"So…Do you want to watch a movie or something?" he asked while washing the pot.

I pictured us snuggled on the couch watching a romantic scene on the television. My face grew hot from the mental image.

"What do you think?" he asked again.

"Uh, okay then," I stammered.

"What kind of movies do you like?"

"I like anything that's not too scary or violent."

"Hmmm…" He stroked his chin. "What's the most scary and violent film I own?"

"Very funny."

Dishes cleaned, dried, and put away, we relocated to the lounge area. Jinseung sat down on the couch. I hesitated, wondering if I should sit next to him, or on one of the other chairs, but he made the decision for me, patting the space next to him. I awkwardly took the spot.

Jinseung scrolled through a selection of movies on the screen. We eventually settled on the romantic fantasy film, Midnight in Paris—one of my favourites.

As the opening credits began, I became hyperaware of Jinseung next to me. I could hear him breathe, feel him adjust his position. I tried to concentrate on the movie.

Shortly into the film, I felt Jinseung's eyes on me. When I looked at him, he averted his gaze, but a few minutes later, I could tell he was staring at me again.

I turned to him and caught his eyes. He didn't look away this time, and neither did I. He chewed his lip in thought as his eyes searched me. My heart pounded on overdrive. He tentatively leaned closer.

29

M y gaze trailed down to Jinseung's lips, which were parted enticingly. Every muscle in me tensed. He moved closer still. I had no doubt about it now—he was about to kiss me. I closed my eyes. Oh so gently, Jinseung's lips brushed against mine.

The sound of the doorbell pierced the air, and I jumped in shock. Jinseung grimaced.

"Who is that?" He paused the movie and got up to view the intercom screen. "Oh? Changsoo *Hyung*."

He opened the door and Changsoo entered balancing several food containers in his arms.

"*Hyung*, what brings you here?"

"Didn't you get my message? I thought I'd bring you some food seeing as you just got back and probably don't have anything to eat."

"I've already eaten."

"Eat some more." His eyes met mine, and a look of shock washed over his face. "*Omo*—Actor Chloe…Why are you here?" He looked at me, then Jinseung, then at me again, eyes narrowed.

"I gave her a ride back from Tongyeong," Jinseung explained, casually. "Now we're just hanging out, watching a movie."

"But you never bring women up here…"

"I don't see her that way. She's my colleague, my friend. Can't I bring her here?"

"Hmmm…I suppose so." He didn't look entirely convinced. "What are you watching?"

"Midnight in Paris."

"I love this movie!"

Changsoo put the food containers on the coffee table and plopped himself down next to me on the couch. "You're not very far through. Mind if I watch it too?" He didn't wait for Jinseung's reply, grabbing the remote to resume the movie.

With gritted teeth, Jinseung sat down on another chair.

Changsoo helped himself to the food he brought over, eating noisily while watching the movie. Meanwhile, Jinseung and I exchanged exasperated glances.

If Changsoo hadn't arrived when he did, what would have happened? This thought kept playing through my mind, distracting me from the movie.

As soon as the movie ended, Changsoo announced he would be on his way. "Do you need a ride home, Chloe?" he asked.

"Uh, yes please," I replied.

I couldn't turn his offer down, it would only increase his suspicion, and I didn't want to get Jinseung into trouble.

I said goodbye to Jinseung and followed Changsoo down to the carpark. I hopped into the passenger seat of his rundown car. Changsoo didn't start the engine straight away. Instead, he turned to me and his cheerful demeanour rapidly dissolved, replaced by a side of him I'd never seen before.

"Don't get involved with him, Chloe," he said sternly. "It will only end in tears."

30

I replayed our brief kiss over and over again in my head while I lay in bed, allowing myself to fantasise about what would have happened if we hadn't been interrupted. Eventually my fantasies blurred into dreams.

When I woke up in the morning I reached for my phone, hoping to see a message from Jinseung. As I had wished, a new message awaited me, but my heart dropped as soon as I opened it.

Jinseung: I'm sorry about what happened. The kiss was a mistake.

I didn't make eye contact or say hello to Jinseung when I got in the van. I sat silently in the back seat, arms folded tightly across my chest, seething with fury.

"You're awfully quiet," Bora said. "Everything okay?"

"I'm fine, thank you," I said curtly.

Bora let out a loud sneeze.

"Are *you* okay?" I asked.

"I think I'm coming down with something."

"That's no good."

"You shouldn't be working today," Changsoo said.

"I'm sure I'll be fine," Bora said, right before another sneeze.

I could feel Jinseung's eyes on me the entire car trip, but I ignored him.

Bora interrogated me as soon as we were alone in my dressing room. "Are you mad at Actor Shin or something?" she asked.

"It's…nothing," I said.

She opened her mouth to question me further but started sneezing again.

Jinseung appeared at the door, bearing a box of tissues. "Want one?"

"Oh! Yes, please."

He passed her the box. "Do you mind if I speak with Chloe alone for a minute?"

"Uh…sure." She hesitantly left the room.

"What do you want?" I snapped.

"I can't stand this," Jinseung said in a tone which made it seem like I was the bad guy.

"What? How were you expecting I'd react?"

"I thought you'd be a little more understanding of the situation."

"I was so happy when you kissed me…and then you take it all back. How can I be understanding of that? Was it really a mistake?"

"Yes—I mean, no—I mean…I don't know."

"Did you mean it or not?"

Jinseung's demeanour softened. "I really care about you, Chloe."

I paused, feeling my heart stir with the sincerity of his words. *No. I can't let him off the hook so easily.* "That doesn't answer the question. Was the kiss a mistake?"

He rubbed his neck. "Perhaps I didn't word it so well. What I meant was, I wanted to kiss you, but I probably shouldn't have done it. At least, not yet. I acted rashly in the heat of the moment. I didn't think things through."

I considered his explanation since he sounded so earnest.

"There's a lot I have to think about. Give me some time." He looked at me with pleading eyes.

My anger slowly melted away. "…Okay."

He pulled me into a hug. "I shouldn't have sent you that message. I'm sorry. Can you forgive me?"

"…Yes. I forgive you."

31

I hummed a song absentmindedly, walking across the house to the bedroom. I pushed open the door. That's when I saw it.

I dropped my bag to the floor with a heavy thud, a deafening scream escaping my lungs.

There on the bed, a dead dog, lying on blankets stained crimson with its blood.

I hyperventilated, back against the wall, unable to tear my eyes from the gruesome scene.

"Cut," Nara said. "Thank you. That's all the shots we need."

Slowly, my breathing returned to normal, and I morphed from Louise back to Chloe.

"Bravo!" Jinseung made his way past the crew surrounding me, clapping and cheering. "That was great. Your acting skills have come a long way."

"Thanks," I said, my voice hoarse from all the screaming.

Jinseung stared at the model dog, grimacing. "*Aigoo*, that looks so realistic. It's creepy."

I looked around. "Where's Intern?"

"She wasn't feeling well. I made Changsoo *Hyung* take her home."

"Ah. She did seem sick."

"Since *Hyung* isn't back yet, I guess you'll have to keep me company instead."

I smirked. "Will I just?"

"I left something in my dressing room. Come on, let's go." Before I could protest, he tugged me away from the set and towards the dressing rooms.

Once safely inside his room, he closed the door firmly behind us. I wondered whether he really needed to get something or if he just wanted to get me alone for some reason. Changsoo's warning replayed in my head. "Don't get involved with him, Chloe." Plus, I still hadn't fully forgiven him for telling me the kiss was a mistake.

"Perhaps I should go," I said. "I don't have anything else to shoot today. There's no point in sticking around."

"Stay, please?" He pouted. "It's too boring waiting around by myself."

Damn him and his cuteness. I can't resist that face. "What was it you left here?" I asked.

"Huh? Oh, these." He grabbed a pair of handcuffs off the table.

"Handcuffs? Is that what you need?"

"I have to arrest someone in my next scene." He snapped one of the cuffs closed around his wrist.

"What are you doing?" I asked, laughing. "I hope you can get that off."

Before I could react, Jinseung snapped the other handcuff on my wrist, linking us together.

"Now there's no escape!" he said. "Muahahaha…"

"Arrggh. What have you done?"

I tried to manoeuvre my wrist out of the handcuff, but it was too tight. We were well and truly stuck together.

Jinseung tugged me by the wrist, causing me to stumble. I half shrieked, half laughed.

We continued to mess around, stumbling up and down the room. When Jinseung flopped down on the couch I came tumbling on top of him, right into his lap. "*Omo…*"

Jinseung made no effort to wriggle away. Instead, his lips slowly curled into a wide grin. "No wonder I kissed you. You're so hard to resist…"

I turned my head away. "I won't let you make another mistake."

A loud knock sent us scrambling up from the couch.

"Shin Jinseung, please report to set," an assistant said.

Jinseung sighed. "I guess they're ready for me now. I should go."

"What about the handcuffs?" I asked.

"Hmmm…I wonder how to get them off."

"You don't know how?!"

"I don't have a key. I wonder if there's a button or something." He felt around the cuff.

I also tried to work out a way to open the handcuffs, but my attempts were futile.

At last, Jinseung admitted defeat. "We'll have to go to wardrobe and ask how to get them off."

"Oh, great," I said, dreading the impending walk of shame.

Sure enough, crew members threw us odd stares and chuckles as we made our way up the corridor to the wardrobe area.

The wardrobe *ajumma* looked at us with her eyebrow raised.

"We're stuck in these," Jinseung said.

"I can see that. How did—never mind. I'd rather not know. There should be a spare set of keys around here somewhere…" She rummaged in a drawer and fished out a pair of tiny metal keys. "Ah, here we are."

Jinseung eagerly accepted the keys, but before we could free ourselves, someone spotted us.

Baek Yena stopped in the doorway. She burst out laughing at our predicament. "If you want to play with handcuffs, they have pink fluffy ones designed for that."

I blushed furiously as Jinseung released me.

32

"I can't believe you managed to talk me into this," I lamented.

Bora stood outside the door to my apartment armed with beer and snacks.

"You'll thank me later," she said, removing her shoes and coming inside.

I hadn't planned on watching Hidden History. The very idea of seeing myself on-screen made me cringe with embarrassment. Yet here we were, about to watch the first episode as it aired.

We made ourselves comfortable on the couch. Bora pulled her laptop out of its sleeve.

"Why did you bring your laptop?" I asked.

"To monitor people's reactions online, of course," she replied.

"Ohhhh."

She fired up her laptop and brought up a dashboard of various stats and charts on the screen.

"The search term 'Hidden History' is already trending," she said.

I peered at the screen in bemusement. "Did you set all this up yourself?"

"Yep."

"That's cool."

Bora shrugged. "It's all part of the job. I've got to keep tabs on these things."

As the previous show started to wrap up, I grew increasingly jittery. Teasers for Hidden History played in the ad breaks.

"I'm so excited," Bora squealed.

Meanwhile, I felt like I was going to throw up. *My acting's terrible, I know it is. How can I watch this?*

"You look like you're about to faint," Bora said. "I'm sure it will be fine."

Her words did nothing to reassure me.

The episode began. I watched through squinting eyes, ready to squeeze them closed as soon as I appeared.

Jinseung and Yena lit up the screen as Officer Park and Detective Jung investigating a murder, but I couldn't fully focus being so apprehensive about seeing my scenes. I couldn't even follow the storyline despite my familiarity with the script.

During the ad breaks, Bora opened her laptop and refreshed her dashboard, looking for updated stats and comments. "People seem positive so far," she said. "Lots of Jinseung's fans are watching."

I glanced at the stream of comments coming in through the feed.

"Shin Jinseung is so hot!"

"*Saranghae* Jinseungie! Fighting!"

"🖤 Shin Jinseung 🖤"

While reading the comments, I didn't realise the ad break had already ended. I returned my attention to the television.

We reached the halfway point in the episode and I still hadn't appeared.

"When is your scene going to play?" Bora asked.

I shrugged. "Maybe I was so bad they cut the scene?"

"Don't be silly—" She gasped. "There you are!"

The bar scene played. I held my breath the entire time, waiting for my poor acting skills to be exposed. But it never happened. The scene had been cut in a way that disguised my errors. Eventually the butterflies in my stomach dissipated. Before I knew it, it was over.

"You were so good," Bora said, clapping.

"It wasn't as bad as I thought it would be," I admitted.

"It wasn't bad at all! You're way too hard on yourself."

With my first scene out of the way, I allowed myself to relax and enjoy the rest of the episode.

"Our Jinseungie is so good-looking in police uniform," Bora mused, crunching into a *tteokbokki*-flavoured snack.

"He sure is…" I agreed, thoughts turning to our recent handcuff escapade in the dressing room.

"What are you smiling about?" Bora asked.

"Oh, nothing!" I snapped out of my daydream.

My next scene came up sooner than I expected and I momentarily cringed, but like before, I eased into it, realising it wasn't so bad.

It felt strange to watch myself with Jinseung. The way he looked at me, or rather, the way that Officer Park looked at Louise, made me blush.

"Your chemistry with Jinseung is amazing!" Bora gushed.

"You think so?"

"Definitely. I'm so glad that writer-nim decided to include a loveline."

"I wonder what the viewers will think…"

"We don't have to wonder." Bora brought up her dashboard again and scanned through the comments. "Hmmm… not much to go off yet, but people are searching 'Hidden History Louise'. They must be curious about you."

After a few more scenes, a cliffhanger marked the conclusion of the episode. An immense sense of relief washed over me as the credits rolled. I wasn't terrible. I hadn't made a complete fool of myself with my attempt at acting. Everything was okay.

"There. That wasn't so bad, was it?" Bora said.

"I shouldn't have gotten myself so worked up," I admitted.

I walked to the kitchen and unplugged my phone from its charger. The screen turned on, and I nearly dropped it in astonishment.

"What the…?"

Notification pop-ups filled the lockscreen. I swiped my thumb to unlock it and scrolled through a long notification list of friend requests, new followers, and private messages.

"What's wrong?" Bora asked when I returned to the lounge.

"I've got so many new followers on social media all of a sudden."

"That's to be expected. People were looking you up during the episode."

"What should I do?"

Bora stroked her chin in thought. "Don't respond to anyone right now. There are loads of staff at KAM who help with the actors' social media accounts. I think someone will be able to help you."

I nodded. "Good idea."

"Come to KAM tomorrow and I'll sort you out."

———

On my way to the KAM headquarters the next morning, something strange happened.

I left the subway at Gangnam station and walked along the street minding my own business when a stranger approached me from out of the blue.

"Are you Louise?" the woman asked.

My first instinct was to say no, then I realised she meant my character in Hidden History.

"Yes," I said. "I play Louise."

"Can I take a photo?"

"Sure."

She quickly snapped a shot, thanked me, and walked away grinning.

*That was weird…*I continued on my way, bemused by the experience. I didn't imagine I'd get recognised just from a couple short scenes in the first episode. It was both exciting and unnerving.

When I arrived at KAM, the atmosphere in Jinseung's management office buzzed.

"Overnight ratings are in," a male staff member said. "Hidden History picked up 9.5."

"What does that mean?" I asked.

"It's doing well."

"That's good news!"

Bora waved me over to her computer.

"Check this out," she said.

She loaded a webpage titled "Chloe Gibson Fans."

"*Omo.* What's this?"

"A fan page."

"I have a fan page?"

"Pretty cool, huh?"

The poorly made website featured screenshots of me from the first episode of Hidden History paired with a few other photos of me scraped together from various sources.

"That's kind of cool…kinda creepy too," I said.

"Right?"

After we'd had our fix of the strange website, Bora suggested we head to the PR department to get their intern to help me with my social media. We were about to leave when Changsoo and Jinseung entered the office.

"I didn't expect to see you here," Bora said. "Aren't you supposed to be at an audition?"

"We're heading there shortly," Changsoo said.

"Audition?" I asked.

Jinseung nodded. "I'm up for the lead role in a romantic comedy called Love Apprentice."

"That's fantastic!"

"PD Song has Jinseung specifically in mind," Changsoo explained. "His heartthrob image and young female fanbase makes him a perfect fit for the role. The audition is just a formality. He practically has it in the bag already."

"Don't mess it up by being late!" Bora reprimanded.

Changsoo checked his watch, before running to his desk and grabbing a few bits and pieces. "Right. That's everything. We're leaving now."

"Good luck!" I said.

33

I *can't live in this prison cell*, I thought, examining the tiny bedroom. Dust particles floated in the sliver of dull light cast through the dirty window. A single bed took up most of the floorspace, and although my arms weren't long, when I extended them, I could easily touch the opposite sides of the wall.

"Rent is 800,000 won per month," the property manager said.

"800,000 won?" I repeated in disbelief.

"You won't find better value in this part of town."

I sighed. "No. I suppose not."

Maybe it wouldn't be so bad. It would be a temporary situation, after all. Once I had secured a teaching job, the school would provide me with an apartment.

A rhythmic banging noise started up and the paper-thin walls vibrated.

"What's that sound?" I asked.

The property manager's face turned red and he rubbed the back of his neck nervously. "I'm not sure. It's usually very quiet, I assure you. Anyway, that's all there is to see." He hurriedly ushered me away from the room. "So…are you interested?"

"Hmmm…I'm going to have to say no."

"Okay. Well, if you change your mind, you know how to contact me."

I left the building, dejected. Another failed apartment inspection to add to my list. At this rate, I'd be homeless when I needed to move out of my current place. *Maybe I have to lower my expectations. Maybe I'll have to move out of Seoul.* The prospect of leaving Seoul saddened me, or more accurately, the prospect of leaving Shin Jinseung.

On board the subway home, I checked my phone. A notification of a new email popped up on the screen and I absent-mindedly tapped it open. My heart sped up when I saw it was about one of the teaching positions I had applied for. I quickly scanned the message and one sentence jumped out at me. *Unfortunately, you have not made it through to the next round of the application process.*

Disheartened, I slid down in my seat and stuffed my phone back in my bag. The rejection was upsetting but not surprising. Hiring season wasn't for a few more months. Jobs were limited and competition was fierce, particularly for jobs in Seoul. The little voice in my head repeated my previous thought. *Maybe I'll have to move out of Seoul…*

Hidden History would wrap up soon. Even if I managed to get a job in Seoul, my life would change dramatically. Jinseung and I would be on completely different paths. I might not even get to see him again. And even if by some miracle he decided to risk his career to date me, we wouldn't be able to spend much time together.

Negative thoughts plagued me as I walked home from the

station, home to my apartment I would soon be kicked out from.

Crossing the lobby to the elevator, a familiar face stopped me in my tracks. I rubbed my eyes. *Seri?* She sat on a chair by the post boxes, hunched over with her eyes glued to her phone screen.

"Seri-ya," I said.

She lifted her head at the sound of my voice. Her face brightened.

"*Unnie!*" she cried.

I stared at her in confusion. "What are you doing here?"

"I was just trying to call you. I recently arrived in Seoul and thought I would stop by."

"It's good to see you again."

Her face contorted into a look of concern. "Are you okay? You look totally worn out."

"It's a long story."

———

In a small *jajangmyeon* restaurant decorated with hanging red lanterns, I relayed my various dilemmas to Seri. She listened intently while slurping her noodles.

"You're in a tough situation," she said. "If only Jinseung could be more clear about his feelings for you."

"I feel like I can't move on with my life until I know what he's thinking. Do I have a chance with him or not?"

"Maybe dating a celebrity isn't such a good idea anyway. Think about it. You'd have to deal with jealous fans, relentless media scrutiny, and being in the public eye, not to mention the resentment he might feel if it negatively impacted his career."

"I know all that…and yet, I still think it would be worth it. Am I crazy?"

"No. It's Shin Jinseung after all. I don't blame you."

I rested my head in my hands. "*Aigoo*. He's constantly on my mind these days. I don't know what to do."

"I know what to do."

"What?"

"Let's get drunk."

I couldn't help but laugh. "That's your solution to everything."

Seri ordered a bottle of soju. She poured the clear liquid into shot glasses.

"Cheers," we said, clinking glasses.

I downed my shot. "Ahhhh…I feel a bit better already."

"See. Told you."

We continued to drink, the strong alcohol numbing my incessant thoughts. When we finished our first bottle, Seri ordered another. It didn't take long to polish that off either, and before I knew it, Seri had ordered a third bottle. By our fourth bottle, I was well and truly inebriated.

"You know what?" Seri slurred. "You should just ask him. Ask him straight up whether he wants to date or not."

"I can't do that!" I said. "If I put pressure on him, I'm sure he'll just say no."

Seri frowned. "Yeah…that could be true."

I let out a wistful sigh. "I wish I could see him right now. He lives in this area, you know."

"Hey! I've got an idea!"

"What is it?"

"Pass me your phone."

I unlocked my phone and handed it over. She started to tap at the screen with a conspiratorial look on her face.

"What are you doing?" I asked.

"Shhhh!" She pressed the phone to her ear, a mischievous smirk on her face.

"Who are you calling?"

She didn't answer me. And then, whoever she had called must have picked up.

"*Oppa!*" Seri said.

My face grew hot. "Is it Jinseung?"

34

I tried to grab the phone away from Seri, but she evaded.

"It's Seri, Chloe's friend," she explained to Jinseung. "We're drunk!"

I tried to snatch the phone from her again, but she deflected me and I fell off my chair with a crash.

Seri continued her conversation while I gathered myself. "Look, we need a ride home, okay? We're too drunk. Chloe's practically passed out right now. I'm worried about her. Come soon, okay?…We're at Masitda Jajangmyeon restaurant… Okay, bye!" She hung up and passed my phone back to me. "He's on his way. You know what his car looks like, right? He'll call you when he's here."

"He's actually coming?"

"Of course!"

I fanned myself, suddenly dizzy. We went to the counter to settle the bill, but I was so drunk I couldn't even count my money.

"Don't worry," Seri said. "I'll pay."

"But I'm older than you," I spluttered.

Seri laughed. "You sound like a Korean." She paid the bill.

"Thanks."

"No problem. Have a good night, okay? Bye!"

"Bye—wait a minute! You're leaving?"

"I'm not going to be a third wheel."

"How are you getting back to your accommodation?"

"It's just down the road. Don't worry about me!"

"Wait, don't leave me!"

Seri ignored my plea. She smiled and waved before exiting the restaurant.

I slumped back down onto a seat to wait for Jinseung's call. Although I expected it, the sound of my ringtone still startled me. I picked up.

"I'm outside," Jinseung said.

"Coming!"

I hurried out the door and saw Jinseung's car waiting out front. I stumbled into the passenger seat. Jinseung stared at me with a mixture of concern and amusement.

"Are you okay?" he asked. "Where's Seri?"

"She left." I hiccupped and covered my mouth in embarrassment.

Jinseung studied me. "I've never seen you this drunk before." He pulled out into the flow of traffic.

"I'm sorry, *Oppa*."

"What for?"

"You didn't have to come get me. I tried to stop Seri from calling. Are you annoyed?"

"Not at all. I want to make sure you get home safe and sound. In fact, I'm glad she called me."

I broke out into a smile. "Really? You're so sweet!"

Jinseung smirked. "Am I?"

I nodded.

We approached an intersection.

"Now, how do I get to your place?" Jinseung asked.

I gave him directions as best as I could, but we did end up making a few wrong turns along the way.

Finally, we arrived outside my apartment building. That's when I reached for my bag and discovered with a sinking feeling that I didn't have it. I groaned.

"What's wrong?" Jinseung asked.

"My bag. I must have left it at the restaurant."

"Can you go back and get it tomorrow, or do you need it now?"

"My key card is in there. I won't be able to get into the building without it. Reception is closed at this time of night."

Jinseung sighed before making a U-turn and heading back in the direction of the restaurant.

"I'm sorry," I repeated.

When we arrived back at the restaurant, a closed sign hung on the door.

"Maybe you could knock. There must be staff still inside," Jinseung said.

My body swayed as I opened the car door and I nearly fell over on the road.

"Never mind. Stay in the car." He tugged me back inside before pulling out again.

"But my bag!" I wailed. "Where are we going?"

"My apartment."

"Oh! Your apartment is so nice."

"Uh, thanks."

A short drive later, we arrived in the underground carpark of Jinseung's apartment building.

"Wait there," Jinseung said, getting out of the car. He opened the door for me and let me lean on him like a crutch as

I got out. He guided me to the elevator, his arm around my waist.

I looked around confused when we entered his apartment.

"Why are we at your apartment?" I asked, dazed.

"You can stay the night here, since you're locked out of your building."

I gasped. "But what about the rule? You can't break the rule!"

"What rule?"

"No staying the night. Remember?"

Jinseung sighed. "Under these circumstances, the rule doesn't apply."

"Ooooh…So we're spending the night together?"

"Uh, well, not—"

Suddenly, throwing myself at him seemed like a great idea. I flung my arms around him.

Jinseung gently peeled me away. "You're drunk."

I pouted. "You're no fun."

"Sit down. I'll get you a glass of water."

He settled me on the couch then brought over a large glass of water. "Drink up."

I gulped it down in no time flat, then lay my head down, yawning.

"Do you want to go to bed?" Jinseung asked.

I had never heard him say anything so erotic.

"Bed?" I repeated suggestively.

"Don't get any ideas. I'll sleep on the couch. You can sleep in the bedroom."

He opened the door to his room and ushered me through.

I marvelled at the space I had caught a glimpse of only briefly on my last visit. Dark wooden bedside tables, a desk, and a bed with a quilted headboard, grey linen, and black silk pillowcases furnished the classy room. A framed abstract art print hung on the wall.

Jinseung closed the window and pulled the curtains. "Sleep well, Chloe. Goodnight."

"Goodnight."

He left the room, closing the door behind him.

I crawled under the blanket fully clothed. His bed felt incredibly soft and warm, and it smelled just like him. I fell asleep quickly.

Later in the night, something strange happened. A noise jolted me awake and I saw the door open. *What's going on?*

Jinseung walked into the room and got into the bed next to me.

35

Is this a dream? I wondered. *I like where this dream is going…* But as he got into the bed, I realised that it wasn't a dream. "What are you doing?" I asked.

Jinseung grunted. His eyes were closed, and he didn't appear to be lucid. I shook him several times, but he was completely out to it. I gave up trying to wake him. *Maybe I should go sleep on the couch…*

I stared at Jinseung's sleeping form, transfixed. He was only half covered by the blanket. He wore nothing but a thin grey t-shirt and black, form-fitting boxer shorts. My eyes trailed down his enticing figure. *He won't notice if I just cuddle up to him for a bit.* I cautiously edged closer, but at the slightest movement, Jinseung turned over with a groan and draped his arm across me. *This is nice…*I let him hold me in his sleep and soon enough I drifted back to sleep as well.

I didn't wake again until the sound of a blaring alarm in the morning. My head pounded and my throat was dry. "Ow, my head," I murmured.

"*Omo*!" Jinseung jumped out of bed, then realising he was just in his boxers and t-shirt, shielded his crotch with a pillow. "How did I get here?" he asked groggily.

"You walked in during the night. You must have been half asleep."

"Ugh. I must have instinctively walked back to my room after getting up to use the bathroom. I'm sorry…But why didn't you wake me up?"

"You sleep like a log. I tried to wake you up, but I couldn't, and I was too tired and drunk to get up."

Jinseung ran a hand through his hair. "I didn't do anything…weird, did I?"

"No." *Apart from putting your arm around me…*

He exhaled a relieved sigh.

"What time is it?" I asked.

"Five o'clock. I need to get ready for today's shoot."

I staggered out of bed. "I'll leave you to it."

"Help yourself to whatever's in the kitchen if you want something to eat or drink."

"Thanks."

I walked to the kitchen and halfway through pouring myself a glass of water, the intercom buzzed. I froze in panic. No one could know I was here.

Jinseung emerged from his room, flustered. "It must be Changsoo *Hyung*. Why is he so early? Quick, hide in the ensuite."

I hurried through the door on the left side of the bedroom, past a walk-in wardrobe, to the ensuite bathroom. I locked myself inside.

The bathroom was sparkling clean, and the bathtub and shower were huge and fancy-looking. A glass display cabinet housed a wide array of skincare products—bigger than my own collection. I supposed that as a celebrity, he must have to take good care of his appearance.

I examined myself in the mirror, grimacing. I hadn't removed my makeup the night before and its remnants were smeared all over my face. I splashed some water on my face and tried to clean it off.

I sat down on the toilet seat with a sigh. I recalled with embarrassment how I threw myself at Jinseung last night. I wondered if his opinion of me had gone down. My drunkenness couldn't have been at all attractive.

I waited several minutes, unsure whether Jinseung and Changsoo had left yet or not. When I pressed my ear against the door, I couldn't hear anything and decided it was safe to leave. I carefully opened the door and ventured through the wardrobe, back into the bedroom. Again, I pressed my ear to the door. Silence. Slowly, I turned the doorknob and peered through the crack into the living area. *They're gone.*

Alone in Jinseung's apartment, I made myself a coffee.

As much as I wanted to go back to bed, I couldn't risk it. What if someone else showed up at the apartment? A cleaner, or someone from work? Besides, I needed to get my bag back from the restaurant. Someone could be trying to contact me.

I set out, not one hundred percent sure of the exact location of the restaurant, but with enough wandering I found it. It was still closed, but I figured there must be staff inside preparing for breakfast. I knocked on the door.

An elderly lady answered after my second knock. "What can I do for you, *Agassi*?"

"I left my bag here last night," I explained.

"I see. Can you describe it?"

"It's a black leather crossbody with silver hardware."

"Oh! I think I have seen it. I'll go get it for you."

She disappeared then re-emerged holding the bag. "Is this it?"

"Yes! Thank you."

Once she had handed over the bag, I checked through it to see whether everything was still there. I relaxed when I discovered that nothing had been stolen. But my luck ended there. Jinseung called me later in the day with a shocking announcement.

I was in my apartment, scrolling through a job board on my laptop, when my phone started ringing. When I saw that it was Jinseung, a fresh wave of embarrassment washed over me, thinking about how I behaved in front of him last night. I nervously picked up the call. "*Yeoboseyo*?"

"Changsoo knows," Jinseung said, voice solemn.

"Huh? What does he know?"

"That you were in my apartment this morning."

"What?! But how?"

"In my rush, I forgot to hide your shoes. He must have seen them. We had a huge row. He thinks we're dating. I explained what really happened, but he didn't believe me."

"Oh no…What does this mean?"

"Well, he's not happy about it, but I managed to convince him not to tell Mr. Kim."

"That's a relief."

"He says we have to keep our relationship a secret."

"Perhaps we should stop seeing each other outside of work. I don't want to get you into any more trouble."

He reacted swiftly to my suggestion. "No."

"…No?"

"I want to keep seeing you. In fact, as soon as I have some

time off, I want to meet up with you. There's something I want to tell you."

"Can't you tell me now?" I implored.

"No. This is something I want to say in person."

My pulse sped up. *Could it be?*

36

I've been stood up, I finally realised, sitting alone in the private room of a bar with two empty cocktail glasses in front of me.

My hopes had been so high for this meeting with Jinseung. I had spent the last few days fantasising, dreaming, praying, wishing, hoping that Jinseung would confess his feelings to me. But it had all been for nothing. *He's not even coming.*

I tried to call him, but it went straight to voicemail. I texted him again, but he didn't reply. *Did he forget? No, that can't be it…*

Ready to give up, I exhaled a deep sigh and peeled my eyes away from my phone, tucking it away in my bag. I slumped over, laying my forehead on the table in defeat.

"What are you doing?"

I shot up, startled.

Jinseung had arrived. He appeared windswept and flustered, colour in his cheeks.

"You're here," I croaked.

"I'm so sorry. I would be banging my head against the table too if I were you. I know it's no excuse, but I got held up. First, Changsoo decided to engage me in a lengthy conversation I couldn't get out of, and then, I got accosted by fans on the way here. And my phone is dead. You must have been trying to reach me."

My annoyance dissolved. Just seeing him again was enough to warm my heart and erase all my concerns. "It's all right. You're here now."

Jinseung sat down opposite me. "Thanks for waiting. I wouldn't have blamed you if you'd left already."

"I was about to."

"I'm glad you're still here. Can I buy you another drink?"

"Yes please. But better make it a mocktail." Getting drunk and making a fool of myself in front of him again was not on my agenda for the night.

He called over a staff member and ordered a beer for himself and a virgin raspberry mojito for me.

Drinks on their way, Jinseung leaned in across the table and ran his eyes over me. "You look very pretty tonight."

I blushed and pulled my hair back behind my ear. "Thanks. So do you."

Jinseung smirked. "I look pretty?"

"Cute, I mean. Handsome."

"…Sexy?"

"That too."

His smirk widened into a hearty grin. "So…I have some good news."

I raised an eyebrow. "What is it?"

"I found out this morning that I've been offered the lead role in Love Apprentice."

I gasped. "That's brilliant!"

"It's a pretty major step up in my career."

"Congratulations. I'm really happy for you."

"It still hasn't quite sunk in, to be honest."

"One day soon you'll be getting more offers than you can accept, I just know it."

"Thanks. I really hope so."

Our drinks arrived. I took a sip, the sweet, fruity mixture cooling my throat.

"Can I try some?" Jinseung asked.

"Sure." I pushed the glass towards him.

He sipped the drink. "Tastes like raspberry."

I rolled my eyes. "No kidding."

"Refreshing." He slid the glass back to me. "How are things with you, anyway? How's job hunting?"

I sighed. "Well, I hate to be a downer, but not so great. There's a lot of competition for positions in Seoul, and I've only managed to get one interview. It seemed promising, but I didn't end up getting the job. I'm starting to get worried. Soon, I'll have to move out of my apartment, and I don't know where I'm going to live or what I'll do."

"Can't you just stay on at your current place?"

"No. It's too expensive. I can only stay a few more weeks at most. It's funny, but I didn't actually make much money from being in Hidden History."

Jinseung crossed his arms in outrage. "That's not funny! KAM probably gave you terrible terms."

"I know. I didn't have time to go over the contract properly."

"KAM have treated me well over the years, but they'll still rip you off if they have the chance. Just like all the other entertainment companies."

"There's nothing I can do about it now."

"I suppose not, but maybe I can help you on the accommodation front. I own another apartment and it's going to be vacant soon. You could stay there for a while until you sort yourself out."

I considered Jinseung's offer, but it didn't feel right. "That's very generous, but it's too much for me to accept."

"Let me help you."

"I don't want to have to rely on anyone."

"Ah, I see. I can respect that. But if you change your mind, let me know."

"Thanks. Sorry for making you listen to me whine."

"Not at all. I want you to be able to share everything with me. The good and the bad."

I rubbed my fingers up and down the stem of my glass in thought. I couldn't wait any longer. The suspense was killing me. "*Oppa…*"

"Yes?"

"What was it that you wanted to tell me?"

Suddenly he was tongue-tied. "I…hmmm…I don't know how to say this properly."

"It's okay. Just say what's on your mind."

He scratched his head. "So, we kissed a while ago…"

"Yeah…"

"And I still wasn't quite sure if that was a mistake or not. I mean, I loved it, but—"

"I know. Things are complicated for you."

He nodded. "But I've been thinking it over and…"

"And?"

"I've made up my mind. After filming finishes, if it's okay with you, I want to keep on seeing you."

My heart did a somersault in my chest. "That's okay with me. More than okay."

"I'm feeling more open to the prospect of dating now. But let's take it slow. Let's wait until after Hidden History and things are more settled."

I nodded. "Let's take it slow."

Jinseung smiled. "I'm glad you agree."

So, he wasn't going to date me *yet*, but the fact he had warmed up to the idea was more than I ever expected. *It's only a matter of time*, I decided.

"Does this mean you like me?" I asked coyly.

Jinseung reached below the table and took my hand in his. The affectionate gesture made my heart pound.

"Yes, I like you," he said.

"Didn't you say you were over your high school crush?"

"I am over it, but now I have a new crush. This time I know you much better. I'm attracted to you in a completely different way. I really like you as a person."

I smiled, blushing. Jinseung grinned back.

"Do you like me?" he asked.

"Yes, I do."

"I'm so happy to hear that."

We spent the rest of the evening drinking, chatting, laughing. Time flew by and eventually we had to call it a night. We left through a private back exit into a quiet carpark. A single streetlamp shone down on us.

"When will I see you again?" I asked.

"I don't know. As soon as possible." He glanced around the carpark. Upon determining that we were completely alone, he pulled me into his arms and hugged me. I relaxed my head against his solid chest and breathed in his scent.

Just as we were breaking away, I thought I saw movement out of the corner of my eye. "What was that?"

"Huh?"

"I thought I saw something."

I looked around, but there was nothing there. "Never mind."

Jinseung squeezed my hand. "Goodnight, Chloe."

"Goodnight."

37

Bora: How could you do this?

I had just woken up and reached for my phone, only to be confronted by this strange message. I rubbed my bleary eyes and read it again, confused. Unable to make sense of it, I texted her back.

Chloe: What are you talking about?
Bora: Don't play dumb.
Chloe: ???

I waited for Bora to respond, but in the meantime, I received a call from Changsoo.

"You need to come to headquarters and talk with Mr. Kim," he said, voice stern.

"Is something wrong?" I asked.

"Have you not seen the news?"

"What news?"

"I'll send you a link. Read it and report to Mr. Kim's office as soon as possible. Jinseung is already on his way."

Jinseung? Did this have something to do with him as well? A sense of panic unfurled in my stomach.

Changsoo hung up. I received a message from him shortly, containing a link to an entertainment news website. I opened it, hand shaking, wondering what I was about to see. The headline struck me first.

Shin Jinseung Dating Scandal? Exclusive Photos

My heart dropped from my chest to the pit of my stomach. I took a deep breath, bracing myself before I read the article.

Exclusive new photographs show actors Shin Jinseung and Chloe Gibson, co-stars in currently airing drama Hidden History, leaving a bar in Gangnam after a romantic date together.

The couple were caught on camera sharing a hug and holding hands outside the bar. Exclusive photos below.

Shin Jinseung and Chloe Gibson are both represented by KAM Entertainment. A statement has yet to be made on the status of their relationship.

I remembered our hug the night before and how I had seen movement nearby. There must have been someone there, hiding. I wondered whether a worker at the bar might have tipped off a reporter, then the reporter could have hidden and waited for us to leave, camera at the ready. *We should have been more careful.*

Several photographs accompanied the article. They showed Jinseung and I leaving the bar, talking with one another under the streetlamp, hugging, and Jinseung holding my hand. In the

Korean entertainment world, this was very incriminating evidence of secret dating—a betrayal of the trust of thousands of possessive fans.

My stomach twisted with nerves as I made my way to KAM headquarters, wondering what Mr. Kim had in store for me and Jinseung. Would he ban us from dating each other? Ban us from even seeing each other? I had heard stories of such things before. My mind reeled with endless horrible possibilities.

When I arrived at Mr. Kim's office, Jinseung and Changsoo were already there sitting on the couch with heavy expressions on their faces. Mr. Kim looked grave, a stark contrast to his usual chirpy persona.

"You're here," he said.

His serious tone sent a wave of fear through me.

"I got here as fast as I could, Mr. Kim," I stammered.

"Do you understand the current situation?"

I nodded.

"While neither of your contracts stipulate no dating, it has always been made clear that relationships should only be pursued with utmost discretion. We cannot tolerate this kind of public behaviour. It may be good publicity for Hidden History, but it's not good for the development of Jinseung's career at this crucial juncture."

"I understand."

"I have already heard Jinseung's explanation for those photographs, but I'd like to hear your side of the story."

Jinseung eyed me nervously, his face pale. I had to be careful with my words for his sake. "Jinseung and I have become close friends. We met up for a few drinks, that's all."

"And the hug? The hand holding?"

"Where I'm from, those things aren't a big deal. Friends hug and hold hands all the time. It doesn't mean anything."

Mr. Kim thought this through for a moment then visibly eased, his posture slackening. "I believe you. But in Korea, people will get the wrong idea. You're a foreigner and you don't understand how things are done around here, so I'll let you off the hook this time."

"Thank you, Mr. Kim."

"But this cannot happen again in future."

"Yes, Mr. Kim."

He turned to Changsoo. "Manager Bong, get your team to prepare a press release explaining that Chloe and Jinseung are friends, nothing more."

Changsoo nodded and made a note in his diary.

Mr. Kim continued, eyes on me and Jinseung. "From now on, you two are strictly not allowed to see each other outside of work, and at work, you will not be left alone together. And one more thing. Jinseung, hand over your phone."

Jinseung reluctantly passed Mr. Kim his phone.

Mr. Kim put the phone in his desk drawer and locked it. "This phone is confiscated. You'll be provided with a new phone with a new number. You are not to share numbers with each other. You have no need to contact each other directly. If you need to get in touch, then Manager Bong and Intern Yang can pass on your messages."

I flinched at the swift and heavy blow. Jinseung looked devastated too, his face drawn and his eyes downcast.

Mr. Kim dismissed us from his office, but we weren't free yet. Changsoo took us aside to continue scolding us.

"I knew this would happen!" he spat. "I should have told Mr. Kim as soon as I started getting suspicious."

He went on and on yelling at us, cursing us for our stupidity.

"Mark my words, I'll be strictly enforcing Mr. Kim's conditions," he said.

Jinseung and I sat in silence, absorbing blow after blow from Changsoo until a phone call finally interrupted his lengthy tirade.

"I have to take this," he said, calming himself.

Jinseung and I exchanged relieved glances, welcoming a moment of reprieve. But reprieve quickly turned to apprehension. As he listened to the mystery caller, Changsoo's features twisted into a look of severe distress.

38

"No…" Changsoo's voice quavered. "You can't do that. We were about to reach an agreement…The rumours aren't true. We're about to release a statement."

My stomach turned at the mention of rumours. Did this have something to do with the dating scandal?

"Please," Changsoo continued. "This will all blow over. Can't you just give it a few more days' thought?"

His pleas didn't seem to convince the caller. Eventually he hung up in defeat.

"I need to speak with Actor Shin alone," he said.

"Of course." I bowed before leaving the room.

As Changsoo and Jinseung privately conversed, I paced up and down the hall, wondering what the call was about. I had an extremely bad feeling about it. Lost in thought, I bumped straight into Bora.

"Intern—" I started.

"Actor-nim," she said coldly, glaring at me with rage-filled eyes.

"I—"

"I hope you have learned your lesson. Jinseung's fanbase is up in arms over what you've done." Her voice shook. "But worst of all, you kept it all from me. I thought we were friends, but maybe I was wrong."

"Look," I began, then shook my head. Now was not the time to try and explain myself. I had a much more pressing concern. "Do you know what's going on? Manager Bong just got a phone call which made him very upset."

Bora softened. "No. I haven't heard anything."

"He's in there talking with *Seonbae*."

"Hmmm…"

Curious, Bora moved closer and turned her ear towards the door. I joined her but couldn't hear anything except snatches of conversation.

"…Knee-jerk reaction…"

"…I'll try to reason with them…"

"…No use…"

We leaned in closer, pressing up against the door, then quickly backed away when it swung open. Jinseung stormed out of the room, face pale and eyes red.

"*Oppa!*" I called after him, but he ignored me.

Changsoo appeared in the doorway, a heavy look on his face.

"What's wrong, Manager-nim?" Bora asked.

He drew a deep breath. "I suppose you'll find out sooner or later, so I'll tell you now… His offer for the lead role in Love Apprentice has been withdrawn."

I stumbled backward in disbelief. "W-what? They can't do that, can they?"

"I'm afraid it's entirely within their rights. We were still in negotiation and no contract had been signed yet."

"Why would they do that?" Bora asked. "Actor-nim is the best fit for the role. PD Song specifically had him in mind—"

"PD Song doesn't want a lead actor who has recently been involved in a dating scandal."

His words exploded like a bomb ripping through every cell of my body. I started to hyperventilate.

Bora looked at me, concerned. "Are you okay?"

I apologised then ran to the bathroom, too upset to hear anything more.

Locked in a toilet cubicle, tears cascaded from my eyes and sobs heaved from my throat.

Jinseung lost his part in the drama and it was all my fault. If we didn't meet on that day… If we hadn't stood outside the bar together…

It finally sank in why Jinseung couldn't, shouldn't date me, or anyone else. His career was his priority right now. He had made that abundantly clear.

The dating curse is real.

———

"You're not good enough for Jinseung!"

"Shin Jinseung should be with a Korean girl."

"What gives you the right to think you're entitled to Jinseung?"

"Give Shin Jinseung back!"

"Whore."

The nasty comments poured into my social media channels through the night. An unstoppable flood. Unable to bear it, I deleted all the social media apps off my phone then tried to go to sleep.

I couldn't get out of bed the next day. When the intercom

buzzed, I ignored it. When it buzzed a third time, I slowly staggered out of bed and made my way to answer it. I saw Bora on the screen and let her in.

"You look terrible," she said, looking me up and down.

"I feel terrible."

"I came to deliver these." She held up two scripts. "The final two episodes. I thought you might not be up to coming into work today—nor should you. There's a mob of angry fans and reporters outside KAM HQ. It's best you lay low for a while."

"*Omo…*"

"Don't worry about it too much. It will all die down in a few days. Just wait and see."

I sighed. "You're probably right."

"The social media team is in the midst of deleting the negative comments off your accounts too."

"That's a relief. Do you want to come in? I'm going to make some tea."

She nodded and stepped into my apartment. "So…how are you holding up?"

"Not very well," I admitted, flicking the kettle on.

"The news about Actor Shin…it really hit you hard, didn't it?"

"I feel so bad for him. It's all my fault."

"No one blames you—"

"Manager Bong does. It was written all over his face."

"That…may be so, but only because he's very protective of Actor Shin. Overly so. He's been his manager for so long. They're like brothers."

As I prepared two cups of tea, Bora shuffled on her feet. "*Unnie*…I'm sorry about the things I said to you. I was just so angry…"

"You have every right to be angry."

"But I never sought to listen to your side of the story."

"If you want to know the truth, I'm willing to share it now."

"So, what is the truth? You're dating him, right?"

"Let's sit down."

I brought over the two cups of tea and set them down on the coffee table. Bora and I sat side by side on the couch.

"I'm not dating Shin Jinseung," I said.

"Really?"

I nodded. "But I can't deny that we're not interested in each other. I really hoped that we would start dating soon after Hidden History. He said that he was open to it, but he wanted to take things slow."

"I wish you had told me."

"I was only just coming to terms with it myself. And then this happened…"

"What are you going to do? Have you spoken with him?"

I shook my head. "I'm probably the last person he wants to speak to right now."

"I'm sure that's not the case—"

"I cost him a job. I got in the way of his career. This was the reason why he said he doesn't date. How can we possibly be together now? He won't want to continue seeing me. We'll have to break things off."

"Is that what you want?"

"No, but I can't see any other option."

"You should discuss this with him."

"How? We can't see each other alone right now, or even talk on the phone."

"I can help you." She took out her phone and sent me a

message. "It's his new phone number. Don't tell anyone that I gave it to you."

"I won't. Thank you." I saved the number under a code name—Buster.

"Give him a call when you're ready."

I nodded.

When we finished our tea, Bora prepared to leave. She paused before reaching the door, a thought striking her. "I almost forgot." She rummaged in her bag and fished out a cap, a pair of sunglasses, and a face mask. "Take these. Like I said before, it's best you lay low for a while and call me if there's anything you need. But if you absolutely must go out, keep a low profile."

"Thank you."

"If you need someone to talk to, remember that I'm here."

"I'll let you know how everything goes."

"Bye, *Unnie*."

"Bye."

On Bora's advice, I didn't leave my apartment for the rest of the day. I attempted to call Jinseung several times, but each time I picked up my phone I felt sick. *I can't do it.*

I didn't work up enough courage to try again until the evening, but just as I picked up my phone it started to ring. The caller was "Buster." Jinseung. *How can it be?*

39

Heart racing, I answered the call. "*Oppa*..." My voice was weak.

"Hi, Chloe," Jinseung answered. He sounded surprisingly calm.

"How did you get my number back?"

"Did you think I didn't write it down anywhere? I knew something like this could happen."

"Oh. I see."

Jinseung paused. I could hear his steady breathing. Eventually he came out with it. "You know I lost the role, don't you?"

Tears gathered in my eyes again. "Yes. I'm so sorry."

"It's not your fault. It was my fault. I let my guard down. I should have known better."

"I feel terrible."

"Don't. Please don't."

"I can't help it. I know how much you value your acting career. I can't bear to think I'm getting in the way..."

"Chloe...It's going to be hard for us to keep seeing each other, you know that, right?"

"Yes."

"That's why I'm starting to wonder if it's better that we don't."

My blood turned cold. I didn't say anything. I *couldn't* say anything.

Jinseung continued. "All the sneaking around, all the secrets…I don't want that for you. You deserve better."

I blinked back tears.

"Chloe? Say something."

"I know," I spluttered. "It won't work. As much as I want it to, it won't work. I won't be happy if your career gets ruined because of me."

"Don't cry. Please don't cry."

"I'm not crying," I lied, though he could definitely hear me crying.

He waited on the other end of the line until my sobs quietened. "Are you okay?"

"Yes."

"Good. I'm really sorry about this."

"It's okay."

"Then…I'll let you go. Goodbye, Chloe."

"Goodbye."

I held back from bursting into tears again until he hung up, then I buried my head in my pillow and wailed. *It's over.*

40

S taring into the empty fridge, my stomach growling, I realised I had two options: leave my apartment or starve. At first, starving seemed like the more palatable option, but eventually the hunger pangs won out. I put on glasses and a face mask to obscure my identity, then made the trek down the hall to the elevator. I had my finger poised on the button, but the door lurched open before I pressed it. Bora stood in the elevator, grasping a large shopping bag bursting with groceries.

"Oh, *Eonni*! Heading out?" she asked.

"Not anymore." I said. "That for me?"

"Yep! I got your message. Sorry I didn't reply. I've been in meetings all day and I only just managed to slip out now."

"That's all right." My stomach rumbled.

"*Omo*. Sounds like you need to eat something right away. Let me prepare you a meal."

"That would be amazing, but are you sure you have time?"

"I can spare the time. After all, looking after you is the most important part of my job."

"You're an angel."

Bora beamed.

Back in my apartment, Bora set about preparing me a ham sandwich and a berry smoothie. "You know," she said, "It's about time you started venturing outside again. The anti-Chloe mob has dissipated and everyone seems to have moved on to the next scandal. Did you hear about it?"

"I haven't been keeping up with entertainment news."

"The idol, Jasper, has been accused of filming secret sex tapes and distributing them amongst his friends. Makes your scandal seem insignificant in comparison, doesn't it?"

"You're right. Thank God I haven't been involved with anything like that. So you think it'll be safe for me to go outside?"

"Yes, but it still pays to be discreet. Hidden History has been growing in popularity—in no small part due to the dating rumour. There's no doubt you will get recognised in public. Avoid crowds, take taxis, not public transport—things like that."

"Okay. Thanks for the advice."

Bora served the meal and sat opposite me at the table. She looked at me with empathetic eyes. "How are you, anyway?"

Her sweet voice, full of concern, was enough to make me crack. Tears welled in my eyes before sliding uncontrollable down my cheeks.

"Oh dear," Bora said, going to my side and wrapping an arm around my shoulders. "Everything will be okay."

"I'm going to have to film my final scenes soon," I blubbed. "I don't know how I'm going to cope seeing Jinseung again."

"Be strong. I know you're capable."

"Thanks," I sniffed.

Be strong...I repeated her words in my head. They would

become like a mantra to me over the next few days, preparing me to face him again.

———

Despite my effort to be strong, seeing Jinseung felt like ripping the band-aid off a wound which hadn't closed up yet. I couldn't bring myself to look him in the eyes as we sat in the van, on our way to film some scenes for the penultimate episode of Hidden History.

An uncomfortable silence reigned, eventually broken by Bora. "What about that whole sex tape saga, eh? That cute little *maknae*…who would have thought?"

None of us responded to her insight.

"Just trying to make conversation," she grumbled. "Sheesh."

As much as I tried to avoid looking at Jinseung I couldn't help but notice the strained expression on his face and the way he kept clutching his stomach. I wondered if he was ill.

"Are you okay?" I asked. "Does your stomach hurt?"

"I'm fine," he said.

He was obviously unwilling to talk about it so I didn't push the subject any further.

———

Filming faced significant delays. Camped out in Jinseung's dressing room, we practiced our lines together, chaperoned by Changsoo and Bora at all times.

"Shall we try it once more from the top?" Jinseung asked.

I nodded meekly and flipped back to the start of our scene.

Despite all that had happened between us, Jinseung's

ability to act hadn't suffered at all. Meanwhile, I could only summon the energy to dredge up a mediocre performance at best. Having spent the last couple of weeks sick with grief, I had barely practiced my lines, nor had I even managed to *look* at the final episode's script.

Over and over again, we practiced episode 15 with no improvement on my part. Eventually Changsoo suggested we move on to episode 16—the final episode.

"Shall we?" Jinseung asked.

"Okay. I haven't practiced any of it yet, though," I warned.

"All the more reason to start working on it now," Changsoo said.

I read from the episode 16 script in my hands, every line completely new to me. The slow-paced episode answered lingering questions and tied up loose ends to create a satis-fying conclusion to the series.

With only a few pages remaining in the script, my final scene appeared: Louise meets Officer Park after the criminals have been sentenced and they take a walk together.

"Now that the criminals have been reprimanded, and my story has been published, I don't really have a reason to stay here," I read.

"You do have a reason to stay here," Jinseung said.

"…What is that?"

"Me. Please don't go. I'm asking you not to go." He had a pleading look in his eyes.

Real tears welled in my eyes. I brushed them away. "I've been waiting for you to say that."

The next words in the script were a stage direction: *Louise and Officer Park kiss.*

I froze. *How can I kiss him now after everything?* I anxiously lifted my gaze to read Jinseung's reaction, but just as I met his eyes he groaned and doubled over, clutching his stomach again. This time his discomfort did not escape the notice of Changsoo and Bora.

"What's wrong?" Bora asked.

"Do you have an upset stomach?" Changsoo asked.

Jinseung winced. "I don't know."

"Where exactly does it hurt?"

He motioned to his lower abdominal area.

"This is no good. We should get you to a doctor."

Jinseung shook his head. "Let's wait until the shoot is over. I'm sure it's nothing."

Bora rummaged in her bag and retrieved a packet of tablets. "Take these," she said, popping two tablets out. She served them to him with a glass of water. "Painkillers."

Jinseung swallowed the pills.

"Are you sure you're okay?" Changsoo asked.

"I'll be fine."

Changsoo didn't seem convinced, but he had no time to persuade Jinseung to leave. A production assistant came to the dressing room to call us onto set.

We relocated to the police station set to prepare for the shoot. A stylist accosted me and Jinseung, fixing our hair and makeup while the crew set up the camera and lighting.

Baek Yena, who was also appearing in the scene, sat on a chair while her manager aimed a mini electric fan at her face to keep her cool.

I kept a wary eye on Jinseung until the shoot was ready to begin. He gave no sign of illness away to the cast and crew.

On Im Nara's signal, the actors took their positions on set.

"Action!" she called.

With the camera following me behind my shoulder, I

approached the police station reception. The actor playing Officer Do looked up and his face dropped in shock.

"I'm back," I said.

He called out to his colleagues. Yena and Jinseung as Detective Jung and Officer Park came running. They stared at me, speechless.

"Surprised?" I asked.

"Cut," Nara said. "Shin Jinseung, someone you love, someone who you thought might be dead, has just returned. You should be overflowing with emotion."

Jinseung nodded.

"And please walk normally. Looks like you're limping slightly? Let's try again."

We started the scene again. At the point when Jinseung's eyes locked onto me, his face turned white. Everyone waited for him to say his line, but he didn't say anything. He had a spaced-out look in his eyes and his forehead was slick with sweat. It seemed like he was about to say something, then his whole body went limp and he collapsed with a loud thump on the floor.

41

"Jinseung!" I screamed, before flinging myself towards his unmoving body. I laid a hand on his cold, clammy forehead. His eyes briefly flickered open and then closed again.

"Stand back!" A crew member wearing a fluorescent vest and holding a first aid kit shooed me out of the way. He crouched down and checked Jinseung's pulse. Upon determining it was okay, he bundled up a jacket and put it below Jinseung's legs to raise them slightly. He also loosened Jinseung's clothes by removing his belt and undoing a few of his buttons.

A siren in the distance grew louder while I watched on helplessly. I shifted anxiously on my feet, heart pounding, eyes wet with tears. Bora stood beside me whimpering.

Murmured questions filled the room.

"What happened to him?"

"Is he okay?"

"Is he dead?"

When the ambulance arrived, paramedics rushed to Jinseung's side.

"He's been experiencing stomach pains in his lower abdominal area," Changsoo explained.

"Thank you. That's useful information," a young female paramedic said.

After checking his vital signs, the paramedics lifted Jinseung onto a stretcher and carried him to the ambulance waiting outside.

"I'll go with him in the ambulance," Changsoo said.

"Can I come too?" I asked.

"Me too," Bora said.

Changsoo shook his head. "There's only room for one person to go. Take the van and meet us at the hospital." He hopped into the back of the ambulance and strapped himself into the chair.

As the ambulance zoomed off, siren blaring, Bora and I bundled into the van. A determined look in her eyes, Bora started the engine and haphazardly sped away. For once, I didn't care about Bora's terrible driving. All I cared about was getting to the hospital as quickly as possible.

"He's going to be okay. He's going to be okay," Bora said over and over like a mantra as she drove.

I desperately wanted to believe her.

At the hospital, Bora didn't park properly and didn't care to correct her mistake. We hopped out and ran towards the accident and emergency entrance.

"We're looking for Shin Jinseung. He just arrived by ambulance," Bora said to the receptionist.

"Are you family?"

"We're colleagues."

We showed her our KAM employee cards.

"Yang Bora and Chloe Gibson…" She checked something on the computer. "I see that you're both approved visitors. You'll find him in room 12. Through those doors, then follow the signs."

Bora and I hastily made our way through the linoleum-floored corridors which smelled of disinfectant.

A security guard stood outside the door to room 12. We explained who we were, then he let us inside.

The immaculate private room had beige walls and a polished wooden floor, a large television, a couch and two armchairs. Jinseung lay on the hospital bed, awake but weak, while Changsoo stood talking to a doctor, an anxious look on his face.

I immediately went to Jinseung's side. "*Oppa*."

Jinseung turned and ran his eyes over me but didn't say anything. His face was pale.

"Is he going to be okay, Doctor?" Bora asked.

"It's suspected appendicitis. We just need to run a few tests to be sure."

"And if it is appendicitis?"

"He'll need to have surgery straight away. The longer it's left, the more likely there could be complications."

Bora joined me at Jinseung's bedside.

"We're here, *Oppa*," she said. "Everything's going to be okay."

Jinseung's pale lips curved into a weak smile.

Bora, Changsoo, and I stayed with him in the room while he underwent various tests. As suspected, the diagnosis was appendicitis. After a brief wait, Jinseung was taken through to surgery.

We sat nervously in the waiting room.

"This is a routine operation," Changsoo assured us, but his voice shook with a tinge of worry.

Time crawled at an agonisingly slow pace while Jinseung's appendectomy was underway. I wasn't someone who usually prayed, but this time I did. I closed my eyes and silently begged God that Jinseung would be okay. I even promised that I would forget all notions of ever dating him—I'd be happy just to see him alive and well again. That's all I could ever ask for.

I didn't get up from the hard plastic chair. My legs were beginning to fall asleep by the time the waiting room doors finally opened. I jumped up to attention as a doctor emerged. My heart thudded in my chest and my hands were tight fists at my side.

"How did it go?" Changsoo asked.

"I'm pleased to announce that the surgery was a success," the doctor said.

The tension in my body slowly drained as relief washed over me.

"But thank goodness he got here when he did," the doctor continued. "His appendix was severely inflamed, and rupture was imminent."

"But he's okay now?"

"He's in a stable condition. He's still asleep from the anaesthetic. We'll keep him in hospital overnight to recover."

"Thank you, Doctor."

A nurse wheeled Jinseung's bed back to his room.

Mr. Kim arrived later with a bunch of flowers. "How is he?"

"The appendectomy was a success," Changsoo said. "He should fully recover in a couple of weeks."

"That is good news indeed."

Bora fetched teas and coffees and we chatted between ourselves while waiting for Jinseung to wake up.

After finishing his tea, Mr. Kim excused himself. "I'm needed back at the office, but let him know I stopped by."

"Will do," Changsoo said.

"Don't stay here all day. You need your rest too."

We all agreed, though I had absolutely no intention of going home. I wanted to stay with Jinseung through the night if I could.

Changsoo and I flanked Jinseung's bed on armchairs at each side, while Bora lay on the couch opposite the foot of the bed. We all jolted when Jinseung made a groaning sound. Changsoo and I leaned over him. He opened his eyes. The first word to come out of his mouth was "Chloe."

42

"Yes, it's me," I said.

Jinseung turned and reached his hand out to stroke my cheek. "You're cute."

I blushed furiously at the display of affection in front of Bora and Changsoo. Clearly the drugs were still affecting him.

Before Jinseung could say anything else, the door opened and his parents entered the room.

"My Jinseungie!" exclaimed his mother as she rushed to him.

His father stood at the foot of the bed, arms folded. Considering how quickly they had arrived from Tongyeong, they must have dropped everything to race here as soon as they got the call.

"He's okay," Changsoo explained. "Just recovering from the surgery. I don't think the drugs have fully worn off yet."

"My poor Jinseungie!"

"Changsoo-ssi, Chloe, thank you for staying with him through all this," Jinseung's father said. He turned to Bora. "I don't believe we've met."

Bora bowed to him. "Yang Bora. I'm an intern at KAM. I've been working with Jinseung for nearly a year now."

"Thank you, Bora-ssi."

"Now that you've arrived, perhaps we'd better leave. It's a bit too crowded in here for five…" Changsoo said.

I didn't want to leave, but he had a point. Jinseung's parents might want some privacy. Bora and I reluctantly agreed.

"C-Chloe…" Jinseung said.

"Oh? Is there something you want to say to Chloe, dear?" Jinseung's mother said. "Do you want to stay here a bit longer, Chloe?"

I looked to Changsoo for permission. He nodded, giving me the go-ahead.

Changsoo and Bora left the room. I stayed with Jinseung, while he vaguely tried to speak to me, but didn't make much sense. Eventually he fell back to sleep.

"I suppose I'll get going then," I said, turning towards the door.

"Wait—I want to ask you something," his mother said.

I stopped.

"Are you dating my son?" she asked.

"No," I said, flustered.

"Is that so? Jinseung denied it too. What a pity. I kind of hoped the rumours were true."

"Really?"

"I look forward to the day Jinseung introduces me to his girlfriend."

"But what about his career?"

"Some things in life are more important, don't you agree, *yeobo*?"

Her husband murmured in vague agreement.

Feeling bashful, I once again edged towards the door. "I should go. I hope his recovery goes smoothly."

"We'll stay in Seoul and look after him until he's better," Jinseung's mother assured me.

"That's good to hear."

With Jinseung left in good hands, I went home.

———

I spent the rest of the evening not quite sure what to do with myself. Seeing Jinseung sick like that had been a shock to my system, and I couldn't shake the memory of him collapsing from my mind.

After a cup of tea, I managed to calm myself down enough to open my laptop and check my emails. Mass emails from KAM and the Hidden History production team had been sent around about Jinseung's appendicitis. Farther down my inbox, another subject line caught my attention—"English Teacher Job Interview". I read the email.

Dear Chloe Gibson,

We have read your resume and would like to interview you for a position at BT Academy in Busan. Could you please confirm a time for a phone call?

Kind Regards,

Alice Kim

My initial reaction was to decline the interview and say I was only interested in jobs in Seoul. Then I remembered that I no longer needed to stay in Seoul since I didn't need to stay near Jinseung.

I heaved a large sigh. *Busan*…A nice city, by all means. Close to Tongyeong, so I could see my host parents more often. It wouldn't be so bad to leave Seoul. With this in mind, I confirmed a time for the interview.

43

I didn't see or hear from Jinseung again until filming resumed two weeks later. All remaining scenes of Hidden History involving Jinseung had been delayed until his recovery, and then all shot at once over a hectic three-day period.

Bora had teased him about the way he said my name when he woke up in the hospital, but Jinseung couldn't remember anything from that afternoon.

On the final evening of filming, Jinseung and I stood in our starting positions for the last scene to be shot for Hidden History—the kiss scene between Louise and Officer Park.

Golden hour bathed the leafy park in warm evening light. I shuffled my feet on the concrete pathway, my thoughts heavy with the prospect of leaving Hidden History, leaving KAM, and perhaps never seeing Jinseung again.

"Are you okay?" Jinseung asked. "You look concerned."

"I was just thinking about how this is my last day as a K-drama actor. It's bittersweet."

"Ah, I see. But I'm sure there will be many more opportunities for you in the future. Changsoo said you had an interview for a job at a *hagwon* in Busan?"

"Yes. I've been offered the job. I'm starting next month."

"That's good."

The steadicam operator positioned himself so we were correctly in frame, and an assistant shone light onto us with a reflector. Everyone readied themselves for the first take.

"Action," Im Nara called.

The scene began with Louise and Officer Park taking a walk through the park, chatting about everything that had happened. It had a bittersweet feeling, just like my mood.

We came around a bend in the path then took a seat at a park bench. My heart rate increased, knowing the kiss drew near. We hadn't practiced it at all. My lips tingled in anticipation.

"Please don't go. I'm asking you not to go," Jinseung said, his eyes were fixed on mine.

My face broke into a relieved smile. "I've been waiting for you to say that."

"...I like you."

"Me too."

Jinseung swallowed, studying me with an intensity which made me flinch. Slowly, he moved towards me, the space between us disappearing. He planted a brief kiss on my lips. It felt awkward. Both of us blushed.

"Cut!" Im Nara yelled. "Shin Jinseung, this is the moment viewers have been waiting for. It looks like you're holding back for some reason. Put some more enthusiasm into it."

"Yes, PD-nim," Jinseung said.

I could understand his hesitation. Kissing was difficult in our situation. But we had to put that behind us to make the scene convincing.

We began again from the point where we sat down at the bench.

"I like you," Jinseung said, his breath shaking.

"Me too," I said.

My heart pounded as he leaned in. Slowly, softly, he pressed his lips to mine. This time, he didn't break away so fast, spending time to build and deepen the kiss. Completely mesmerised, I forgot everything else, becoming oblivious to the filming, oblivious to the fact that we were acting.

When Jinseung finally pulled away, reality came crashing back. I could see the crew around us in my peripheral vision, even as I tried to focus only on him. He stared into my eyes with an expression of longing. I couldn't tell whether it was Jinseung longing for me, or Officer Park longing for Louise. We stayed with our eyes locked on each other until Im Nara called cut.

"That's more like it," she said.

We had to kiss several more times so the camera could capture it from multiple viewpoints. I applied lip balm between takes because my lips were starting to get raw and dry. Each time we dove in for another kiss, I felt Jinseung's resistance wear further away.

"And…cut! That's a wrap. Good job everyone," Im Nara said at the end of the last take.

Cheers and whoops erupted all around.

Changsoo and Bora came rushing to us, smiles on their faces. We embraced in a group hug.

"Congratulations, guys! A brilliant end to a brilliant drama," Bora said.

"Good work, both of you," Changsoo said. "I'm so proud."

"Are you crying?" I asked, noticing the tears well in his eyes.

"No. Some dust just flew into my eyes." He wiped his face with his hand.

"Dust?" Bora asked incredulously.

An awkward pause ensued before we burst into a fit of laughter.

"Everyone's heading to a bar now to celebrate," Changsoo said once he had caught his breath.

"Then what are we waiting for?" Jinseung said. "As soon as we're out of these clothes and makeup, let's go."

———

The entire bar had been booked for the event and drinks were free. Cast, crew, managers, and assistants piled inside.

"Shin Jinseung! Chloe Gibson!" Baek Yena called, inviting us to her table. We pulled up a few more chairs to join her, Cho Dongjoo, Kim Jaehyun, and their managers. Yena filled our shot glasses with soju.

"Cheers," she said, clinking glasses with us. "Another drama under wraps."

"Did you hear about last episode's ratings?" Cho Dongjoo asked. "Nearly double digits!"

"It's going even better than I expected," Kim Jaehyun said.

"What's next for you, Chloe? Have you heard of any other roles?" Yena asked.

"I think Hidden History is probably my first and last drama," I replied. "There aren't many roles out there for foreigners like me."

"I keep forgetting that you won't be with KAM anymore..." Bora said. "That's so sad."

"Yeah. We probably won't see each other again."

She shook her head.

"No. Let's stay in touch, no matter what."

"I would like that."

"We're friends, *Unnie*."

"Yes, we're friends."

"I'll visit you in Busan."

We exchanged warm smiles. Yang Bora would no longer be my colleague, but the idea of our continued friendship filled me with joy.

The voices around us began to hush, and heads turned in the direction of Im Nara, who stood on top of a chair to draw everyone's attention.

"I'd like to make an announcement," she said. "I hope you have all kept Friday evening free as requested. In celebration of the success of Hidden History, we will be holding a party at the Domain Hotel for all cast and crew members."

Cheers and applause rang through the venue.

"It's a strictly private event. No press will be in attendance," Im Nara continued. "And the dress code will be formal, so dress up!"

"Chloe, Jinseung-ah, I trust I will see both of you at the party?" Yena asked.

"I'll be there," Jinseung replied.

"Me too," I said. "I wouldn't miss it."

44

Jinseung's jaw dropped when his eyes fell on me across the crowded hotel ballroom.

I had arrived at the wrap party, feeling confident in a long, strapless red dress and high heels.

"C-Chloe," he stuttered. "You look…"

"She looks stunning," Baek Yena cut in, gliding over in a sparkly gown and oversized earrings.

"Thanks," I said. "You look great too. And Jinseung…I haven't seen you in a suit before."

I looked him up and down, admiring the charcoal-grey suit and navy tie, perfectly tailored to his tall, slim form.

"It looks sexy," I said.

"Oh—thank you," Jinseung said. He ran a hand through his hair, suddenly flustered.

A waiter appeared, bearing a tray of wine glasses and an expensive-looking bottle of champagne.

"Would you like some wine?" he asked.

Jinseung and I took a glass each. Yena already had a drink in hand.

"I wonder where we're sitting," Yena said, casting a sweeping glance over the round tables covered with white tablecloths. She checked a sign which showed who was seated where.

"Oh! There we are. We're all sitting at the same table."

People began to take their seats. I joined Jinseung and Yena at a table up front which we shared with several other main cast members.

Prior to dinner being served, Im Nara took to the stage to make a speech. She said thank you to all the main contributors to the series and handed out several flower bouquets and gifts to the important people involved. I had started to zone out when my ears pricked at the sound of my name.

"I'd also like to make a special mention of Chloe Gibson, who stepped up at the last minute, with no acting experience, and did a brilliant, convincing job of Louise," Nara said. "She impressed Writer Kim so much that she wrote her a bigger part than initially conceived. I don't know what we would have done without you, Chloe."

Baek Yena nudged my shoulder and cheered.

I sank into my chair, embarrassed by the mention. I didn't feel like I had done anything particularly special.

Im Nara continued. "Now onto a more solemn note. The actor Tamara Wilson, who was originally cast as Louise, left us to be with her father who she learned was terminally ill. It is my regret to inform you that her father has since passed away. So I'd like you to join me in a minute of silence." She closed her eyes and lowered her head in respect.

Silence fell over the venue.

*Poor Tamara. I was only offered this opportunity thanks to her misfortune…*I couldn't linger on that thought for too long. *It's the work of fate,* I decided.

At the conclusion of Nara's speech, entrees were served—a mouth-watering collection of Korean and Western small dishes.

Between courses, more speeches ensued from people including Kim Eunsook, producers, and executives from the TV network.

After three dinner courses, the music turned up and people began getting up from their seats to mingle and dance.

I stared at Jinseung, who chatted with Cho Dongjoo beside him. *This could be the final night I spend with him…I had better make the most of it.*

"You should ask him to dance," Yena said, noticing my stare.

"Who? Cho Dongjoo?" I quipped.

Yena laughed. "You know who. Hey! Jinseungie!"

Jinseung turned to her. "Yes?"

"Go on," Yena said, winking at me.

"*Aigoo*," I uttered, exasperated.

Jinseung eyed me expectantly.

I had never asked a guy to dance with me before, but what the hell, there was a first time for everything.

"*Oppa*, will you dance with me?" I asked.

Jinseung's lips curled into a radiant smile.

"Sure. Let's go." He took my arm and led me towards the other dancing guests.

"Have fun!" Yena shouted after us.

We danced holding hands to an upbeat song. He twirled me around and did all kinds of funny dance moves, making me smile so hard my face hurt. I allowed myself to forget all that had happened between us and just enjoy the moment. We danced together for another two songs before a male guest I didn't recognise swooped in and stole me away from Jinsueng. He was good-looking, tall, and oozed charm.

"Hey Chloe, my name is Lee Chiwon," he said.

"Chiwon-ssi," I repeated.

I looked over my shoulder back at Jinseung, but he had disappeared into the swarming crowd. Not wishing to be impolite, I stayed dancing with Lee Chiwon until the song ended. By then, another girl had caught his attention, and he left me alone.

Wishing to spend more time with Jinseung, I went in search of him, but got sidetracked by Kim Eunsook who engaged me in a lengthy conversation.

Once I had finished talking with Eunsook, I spotted Yena thanks to her eye-catching dress. I approached her.

"Baek Yena-ssi, have you seen Jinseung?" I asked.

"Yeah. He was chatting with one of the producers," she said. "Probably trying to find out about upcoming projects."

"Ah. I guess I better leave him to it then. It must be important for him to network."

"Chloe, I've booked a suite at the hotel for the night, and I've invited a few people up for some drinks later on," Yena said. "Do you want to come? I'll ask Jinseungie too."

"Yes, I'll come," I replied without hesitation. If Jinseung would be there, I had to be there too.

"Great. You looked so cute dancing with Jinseungie before. You two look so good together. The rumours are true, aren't they? There's something going on between you. I can tell."

"Well, actually…"

"No need to say anything. I understand. Come to my suite at midnight, okay? Room number 1208."

"Got it."

At midnight, I exited the ballroom and took the closest elevator to the 12th floor. Down a maze of corridors, I located room 1208. I pressed the doorbell. Yena opened the door, a grin on her face.

"Come in, come in," she urged.

The gorgeous suite contained a large bed, a sitting area, and floor-to-ceiling windows with magnificent views of the Han River. No one else was in the room except the two of us.

"There's no one else here…" I said. "Am I the first person to arrive?"

"Yes," Yena replied.

She poured me a drink while we waited for Jinseung and others to arrive. A doorbell ring shortly followed. Yena shot up to answer.

"Jinseungie, you made it!" she said.

Jinseung entered the room, his eyebrows knitted with confusion.

"Where is everyone?" he asked.

Yena bit her lip.

"Actually…" she began.

"What?"

"I only invited you two."

"Oh?"

"And I'm just about to head home. You two can use the suite. I know how hard it can be to spend quality time alone together when you're dating. It was the same when I was dating my husband."

"We're not—"

"No need to thank me!"

Before we could do anything, Yena slipped out of the room, leaving us alone in stunned silence.

45

Realisation sank in. *We've been set up.* Jinseung and I stood frozen in the centre of the fancy hotel room, acutely aware of the huge bed looming behind us. We couldn't even meet each other's eyes.

"I wasn't expecting this," Jinseung said at last.

"Neither was I," I said.

"I suppose I should leave…"

"No!"

Jinseung lifted an eyebrow. "What? Do you want me to stay?"

"Well…that's not what I meant. But this could be the last time we see each other. I just wanted to say a proper goodbye."

"I hope things work out well for you in Busan."

"Thank you. I hope your acting career picks up again."

"Then…I guess this is goodbye."

I nodded weakly.

Jinseung opened his arms and beckoned me to him. I stepped closer and he enclosed me in a tight, warm hug. We stayed in that position for what felt like several minutes. I wished he would never let go, but eventually, he dropped his arms.

"Well, I guess I'll be going now," he said.

"Goodbye, *Oppa*."

"Goodbye."

I could have been imagining it, but it looked like his eyes were full of regret.

I felt a painful knot in my stomach as Jinseung reached for the door handle. He turned to me one more time before leaving.

He left me alone in the room. I waited for his footsteps to dissipate before allowing myself to cry. *He's gone. Gone from my life.* The finality hit me hard, destroying the facade of strength I had built up around myself.

Still crying, I walked to the bathroom, stripped the suffocating red dress off my body, and pulled open the glass door to the enormous shower. I turned on the water and submerged myself beneath the powerful flow from the waterfall showerhead.

Why does it have to be this way? Why? I reminded myself that having a girlfriend would hold Jinseung back from reaching his full potential, but for some reason, that idea seemed weak to me now. Jinseung's mother's words echoed in my head: *Some things in life are more important.* I couldn't help but feel that I'd made a huge mistake. *I should have tried harder. I shouldn't have given up on him.* But now it was too late. Jinseung had departed from my life. I cried and cried, letting the shower water mix with my tears and wash them down the drain.

When my skin began to feel tight, I reluctantly turned off the water and stepped out into the steamy room. White towel wrapped around my body, I wiped a hole in the misted-up mirror.

I can't let the night end like this, I thought sombrely, staring at my pale reflection, eyes red and puffy. Then and there, I made up my mind.

Still in my towel, I rushed back into the bedroom and grabbed my phone. I trembled as I pressed the call button. Phone to ear, I waited. *Please pick up.* It rang several times then went to voicemail. I tried one more time. On the first three rings, he didn't answer. Then I heard something strange. The faint sound of a phone ringing outside the hotel room door, and then the doorbell.

I rushed to the door and opened it, forgetting I was just in a towel.

Jinseung stood in the corridor.

"You came back," I said, voice wobbling.

He looked me up and down. The corner of his lips quirked into an amused smile.

I blushed realising I hadn't dressed and pulled the towel tighter around me. "Why are you here?"

He swallowed. "I know it's selfish, but I don't think I can give you up."

My heart leapt. "Then don't."

He stepped forward into the room, pushing me back as he did so. Door closed behind us, he kissed me.

His lips felt warm and soft against mine. I pulled back a little in surprise, and he ran his eyes over me, gauging my reaction before diving in again with more force. He coaxed open my mouth and tasted me with his tongue, drawing shivers up my spine. One of his hands cupped my head, the other held my waist. Deeper, faster, we kissed until we ran out of breath and I broke away, panting. "Jinseung-ah…"

He nuzzled me and said, voice low, "You don't have any clothes on."

"I was so flustered…I wasn't thinking when I answered the door."

There were so many questions I wanted to ask him. Had he changed his mind? Could we be together after all? But I was silenced as he kissed me again. I succumbed immediately, my knees weak. He held me tight against him while vigorously making out with me. His hands explored my body. I dug my fingers into his back and deepened the kiss. Jinseung groaned and pulled off my towel in one swift movement.

I blushed, feeling exposed.

He pulled back to get a better view.

"Beautiful," he murmured, before kissing me again.

As we kissed, I kept my hands occupied by unbuttoning his shirt. My heart beat faster with each opened button revealing more of his muscular chest. When I reached the bottom, he took it off. I ran my hand down his torso. It felt every bit as good as I imagined it would. The body of someone who takes extremely good care of it.

"Let's go to bed." Jinseung's voice was gruff and low.

I nodded, completely at his mercy. He guided me to the bed.

46

B right sunlight burned my eyes when I opened them in the morning.

"Morning, sleepyhead," Jinseung said, his arms still around me.

So it wasn't a dream. Last night really happened.

"Morning," I said, smiling sheepishly. I extracted myself, desperately needing to stretch. My back clicked.

"Did you sleep well?"

"Yes. You?"

"Mmm. I had pleasant dreams for once."

"Did you dream about me?"

"Yes, actually."

"You did? So what happened in the dream?"

Jinseung smirked. "I don't want to corrupt your innocent mind."

"You know I'm not innocent," I retorted.

He chuckled and pulled me closer into his arms. I rested my head on his chest, feeling the rise and fall of his breath. I would be completely relaxed if it weren't for the niggling little question in the back of my mind.

"Are you okay?" Jinseung asked. "You seem a bit tense."

"I…" I wondered whether to bring it up or not. It might spoil the mood.

"What's wrong?"

"I need to know. Where do we stand now? What's next for us?"

"Don't let those things worry you. Let's just enjoy the moment." He glanced at the alarm clock on the bedside table. "There's still enough time."

"Enough time for what?"

"You know…" He leaned in seductively. "We've got this beautiful hotel room for another hour. It would be a shame to waste it."

Despite the concerns plaguing my thoughts, I was unable to resist his magnetic pull. "Well, okay. If you insist."

"I do insist."

He moved closer still. All my muscles tensed in anticipation. Jinseung's eyes bored into me, half-lidded in desire. His lips touched mine, soft and welcoming. He parted his lips and ever so slowly sank into the kiss. His tongue brushed against mine, making me tremble with delight. He groaned and pulled me tighter to him.

Beep beep beep beep.

What the—? I broke away and reached across to the bedside table to grab my phone. I had set a check-out reminder the night before and now it popped up on the screen: Check out 11:00am. *But that's still ages away…*I looked between my phone and the alarm clock and back again.

"*Omo,*" I said.

"What's wrong?" Jinseung asked.

"This alarm clock's wrong. Check out is in ten minutes."

"Wait, are you sure? How could we have slept that long?"

"I don't know."

He checked his own phone. "Gah!"

We scrambled to get up and ready ourselves to leave.

Dressed at last, we only had a few minutes to spare.

"Go home," Jinseung said. "I'll go and check out." He kissed me on the cheek. "Let's meet tomorrow and talk things through, okay? I'll be in touch."

———

Feeling slightly self-conscious in my evening wear, I took the elevator to the lobby then hailed a taxi from outside the hotel.

"Where to?" the taxi driver asked. My head was in the clouds, replaying all the delicious moments in the hotel room, and in my blissed-out state I had forgotten to tell him. I gave him my address.

During the ride home, I sent Yena a text message thanking her for the hotel room. A short moment after I pressed send, my phone started to ring. Yena was calling me back.

"*Yeoboseyo*," I answered.

"So you had a good night, huh? Did you make good use of the room?"

"Uh, yes."

She cackled with glee. "I'm glad to hear it. You and Shin Jinseung make such a cute couple!"

"Heh. Thanks."

"So, are you going to keep your relationship a secret?"

I paused, caught off-guard by her question. "Actually, we haven't discussed anything yet." *Does he even want a proper relationship with me? Was it just a one-night stand?*

"Ah. So you haven't had that conversation."

"I'm a little nervous."

"Don't be. Jinseung's a good guy. I'm sure you'll both come to a sensible solution."

"I hope so."

"If it helps, my husband and I are living proof that a relationship can work between a celebrity and a non-famous person."

"Then…can I ask you something?"

"Fire away."

"When you started dating your husband, did it impact your career? Did you resent him?"

"*Aigoo*. Such heavy questions. Are you worried about Jinseung? The scandal must have hit you both hard. I'm not going to lie, it was hard sometimes. But Dongwoo and I are obviously still together. I have no regrets."

"And your career?"

"I'm still acting, aren't I? Sure, I don't get the same kind of roles as I did when I was a single, hot young thing, but I actually prefer it this way. I'm recognised for my skills as an actor, rather than my looks and single status. I'm taken far more seriously now."

Yena's thoughtful answer lifted an invisible weight off my shoulders. "Thanks. You've clarified things for me."

"I'm glad to be of help. When will you see him again?"

"Tomorrow. I expect we'll discuss things then."

"Good luck."

47

A surprise announcement came from Changsoo the next morning.

"Yang Bora has been promoted!" he said excitedly over the phone.

I was so surprised I fumbled with my phone, nearly dropping it. "*Omo*. For real?"

"Yes. Mr. Kim gave her the good news last night."

"That's wonderful. So what's her new title?"

"I'll leave it to her to explain everything. I'm sure she'll want to tell you the news herself. Are you free tonight? I'm taking her out to celebrate. It would be great for you and Shin Jinseung to come along too."

"Of course! I'll be there."

I was too happy to care that it would disrupt the plans I had already made with Jinseung.

I arrived at a dark underground bar with graffiti art on the walls and Korean hip hop music pumping through the speakers. At a table situated in a corner largely hidden from view, Changsoo, Jinseung, and Bora occupied a small table. I met Jinseung's eyes first and blushed, then quickly diverted my eye contact to Changsoo and Bora.

"Am I late?" I asked.

"Not at all," Changsoo said. "We only just got here."

I took a seat. "Yang Bora-ya, congratulations on your promotion."

She grinned from ear to ear. "Thank you, Chloe."

"So I take it you're no longer an intern, but a fully fledged staff member now?"

"That's right. It's a full-time, salaried position."

"*Daebak*! You deserve it."

"Doesn't she?" Jinseung said. "I've never seen an intern so hard-working and dedicated."

"Just remember to work on your driving skills," Changsoo jibed. "She pranged the van yesterday."

"Thanks again for covering for me!" Bora said sheepishly. "I promise I'll work on my driving."

Changsoo waved over a waiter and we ordered beer, soju, plus a few small dishes to share. Changsoo filled our glasses.

"To Yang Bora," Jinseung said, raising his glass.

"Cheers!" We clinked glasses and downed our drinks.

"Tell us more about your promotion," Changsoo said, leaning in to speak with Bora. "You'll be a manager, right?"

"Yes. I'm going to be a manager for a freshly recruited actor," she explained.

My mouthful of beer went down the wrong way and I started coughing. "Hold on. That means you won't be working with Jinseung anymore," I said when I had regained my composure.

"Correct."

"*Omo*…"

"I know. It's the one thing I'm upset about. But I can't be Jinseung's manager when he has Bong Changsoo."

"Who's the new actor? I don't think I've heard anything," Jinseung said.

"Her name is Go Yoojin," Bora explained.

"Ah yes, Go Yoojin…" Changsoo said. "I think you'll be a good fit for her."

"I guess I'll get to meet her soon," Jinseung said.

"I hear a congratulations are in order for you too, Chloe," Changsoo said.

"Oh?" I wondered what exactly he was referring to.

"Did you not snag a teaching job in Busan?"

"I did." I smiled weakly. The job was yet another thing which stood between Jinseung and I being together, but I decided not to let my thoughts linger on that right then. In the meantime, I refilled my glass. Things would be clearer once I'd talked to him, and I could decide what to do after that.

When we finished our drinks, Changsoo ordered more. Bora filled our glasses, a deliriously happy look on her face.

Should I tell her about Jinseung and I? I promised I would tell her everything, after all.

When Bora got up to go to the bathroom, it was the perfect opportunity. I waited a couple of minutes then excused myself from the table and headed to the restroom. I caught Bora as she left the stall.

"Chloe! How was the party last night? I'm so bummed I didn't get to go."

"I had a great time. Actually…"

"Did something happen?"

I nodded.

"Is it to do with Jinseung?"

I nodded again.

"Tell me!"

"Well, uh, things have progressed in our relationship."

Bora gasped. "Does that mean what I think it means?"

"I think so, yes."

She shrieked with joy. "I'm so happy for you!"

"We still haven't talked everything through yet."

"Busan…"

I nodded. "Among several other considerations."

"You'll work things out with time."

"Yeah. I hope so."

"Anyway, it's fantastic news. I'm so glad you told me. No one else knows anything, right?"

"Yeah. Apart from Baek Yena. She's the one who kind of gave us the final push."

Bora giggled. "She's so meddlesome, but cute. And don't worry about me—I won't tell anyone."

"I know. I trust you."

Bora squealed again, unable to contain her sheer excitement. She had to make a considerable effort to gather herself before we rejoined the others at the table. Apart from a few glances back and forth between us, she managed to conceal her knowledge.

"Another drink, *Seonbae-nim*?" Bora asked Changsoo.

"Yes please."

She refilled his glass.

Later in the evening, Bora suggested we head to a *noraebang*. Within the confines of the karaoke room, she continued to ply us all with drinks, especially Changsoo. I had never seen him so drunk. In fact, I don't think I'd ever seen him drunk at all—he was always the sober driver.

Bora got me up to sing a pop song with her, then Changsoo and Jinseung entertained us with a soppy ballad.

"It's getting late," Changsoo said woozily. "Perhaps I'll leave soon."

I thought Bora would protest, but instead she agreed that was a good idea. After one more song, we said goodbye to Changsoo.

Shortly after his departure, Bora announced she'd be heading off too.

"Are you sure?" Jinseung asked. "We haven't even used up all our time."

"I'm sure. But you two stay here, okay? Make good use of the time left." She flashed me a cheeky grin before leaving.

"What was that about?" Jinseung asked. "Does she know something?"

"Yes," I admitted.

He chuckled. "I suppose that's okay. It's Yang Bora."

"I trust her."

"Yeah, me too."

Our eyes lingered on each other. Jinseung looked so tantalising, biting his lip and surveying me, but we had an important topic to discuss.

"So, about us…are we…" I couldn't get the words out properly.

"Are we a couple now?" He finished for me. "I want you to be my girlfriend. It's as simple as that."

I want you to be my girlfriend. His words echoed in my head and spread a warm, dreamy feeling through my body—but one thing still bothered me. "Why the sudden change of heart?"

He paused in thought. "When I was in hospital I realised something…Ever since I left school, I've been working so hard. I've put work above everything else: my health, my family, my relationships…I don't want to do that anymore. I don't want to deny myself a relationship with you just because my popularity with fans might go down, or I might not get the same kind of acting roles anymore…You're more important to me." He took my hand in his and stroked it tenderly. "In saying that, if you don't want to be my girlfriend, I'd completely understand—"

"I do want to!"

"It's not easy to date someone like me. It won't be a normal relationship. We'll need to keep it a secret—at least in the beginning—and I'm so busy. I won't always have time to see you—"

I always knew there would be downsides and I was prepared to obey all the conditions. "I still want to try."

"You were against it not too long ago."

"I couldn't stand knowing that you lost that role because of me."

"You don't need to feel bad about that."

"Talking to Baek Yena eased my concerns. Once upon a time, she was in a situation just like ours. She and Ko Dongwoo made the choice to be together and she's never regretted it. That made me feel like we have a chance to make this work."

"And Busan? I don't want to stand in your way…"

I shook my head. "There's still time. I can back out of the job and keep looking for a position in Seoul."

"If you're sure."

"One hundred percent."

"Then let's do this. Let's make it work."

Before I could verbalise my agreement, he kissed me. It caught me off-guard and I took a moment to close my eyes and reciprocate, but by then he was already breaking away.

"Chloe…" he said, lips by my ear.

"Hmm?"

"When would you like to go on our first official date?"

48

Our first official date. That's what Jinseung had promised, yet he cancelled our plans and days passed with no further word on that front. Just as I was beginning to get dispirited, a surprise flower delivery arrived to my apartment.

"Chloe Gibson?" the delivery man asked when I answered the door.

"Yes, that's me."

"These are for you." He presented me with the huge bouquet. Beautiful, bright pink peonies.

I accepted it, bemused. "Thanks." I brought the flowers inside, placed them on the table, and fumbled for the message card.

Meet me at Cinema Lumiere, 5pm.

When I arrived at Cinema Lumiere, a note on the locked door read "Closed for a private booking." I stated my name over the intercom and the door clicked open.

Classic movie posters in skinny black frames lined the corridor leading to the lobby which featured leafy indoor plants, a well-stocked bar, and a small sitting area. A large blackboard displayed screening times written in white chalk. A lone woman stood behind the counter flipping through a magazine. Her eyes met mine. She was tall, lithe, and beautiful, with brown dyed hair and green contact lenses, probably in her late twenties.

"So you're Chloe Gibson," she said, a twinkle in her eye. "Nice to meet you. I'm Shin Jina, Jinseung's sister."

"Jinseung's sister!?" I spluttered. I had heard a sister mentioned before, but for some reason it had never occurred to me that I might meet her.

"That's right. He has told me all about you."

"Really?"

She nodded.

"Do you work here?" I asked.

"Yes. I do this part-time and I'm a part-time model."

"So you work in the entertainment industry too…That's cool."

"Yeah, though I'm hardly as successful as *Dongsaeng*—not that I envy him at all. Anyway, go on through to the cinema. He's waiting for you." She motioned to a pair of double doors.

I entered the cinema and gazed around in awe, absorbing my surroundings. The room had been decorated with fairy lights strung across the walls, and candles glowed softly inside cup holders. Jinseung sat in the centre of the back row, a delighted expression on his face as he watched me look around.

"Wow…It's so pretty…" I gushed.

"Do you like it? *Noona* helped me with the decorating."

"It's beautiful. You organised all this for me?"

"Of course. Come here and take a seat."

I ascended the steps to the back row and sat down next to him on the fancy recliner seat. "Comfy!"

Jinseung held my hand in his. "Sorry it's been a while. Things have been busy, as you know."

"I was beginning to think you had forgotten," I admitted.

He shook his head. "How could I? I've been so excited for this."

"Sorry for doubting you. It's clear you put a lot of thought into this date."

"I wanted to make it special for you. I know that the idea of dating in secret is hard, but I wanted to show you that we can still go on proper dates. We just have to improvise a little."

"Thank you. And thank you for the flowers as well. They're lovely."

"I'm glad you liked them. Are you cold?"

"A little."

He reached to his left and grabbed a blanket off the chair.

"Thanks." I draped it over myself and snuggled into its warmth.

"What would you like to watch?"

"What are the options?"

He handed me a programme of new releases, plus some old classics.

"Hmm…"

"What are you in the mood for?"

"Something funny."

After some deliberation, we settled on a recently released romantic comedy. Jinseung notified his sister and brought back an armload of drinks and snacks. As he settled down beside me, the lights turned off and the big screen lit up. He lifted the chair arm between us so we could snuggle up close under the blanket.

The movie started to play. Jinseung wrapped his arm around me and I leaned my head on his shoulder.

"This is nice," he said.

"So nice," I echoed, savouring the closeness between us.

Throughout the movie, our eyes constantly wandered from the screen to gaze at one another.

"Not enjoying the movie?" I asked.

"You're more interesting," Jinseung replied. He pulled me even closer.

"You're distracting."

"Don't you like it?"

"…I do."

"See." He nuzzled me and kissed my neck.

We spent the rest of the movie only half watching. When the credits rolled, a sense of disappointment swelled up inside me. *I should have picked a longer movie, I don't want this night to end.*

"What would you like to watch next?" Jinseung asked, snapping me from my discontent.

"…Next?"

"I have the cinema booked out all evening. There's still time to watch another two movies if you want."

"It seems neither of us can really concentrate on watching movies."

"You know that's not the point. We get to spend all this time together."

I grinned. "Give me the programme."

We watched two more films over the course of the night,

and following that, we hung out in the foyer of the cinema. Jina brought us over dinner from the restaurant next door.

"Delicious!" I exclaimed after swallowing my first mouthful. Despite constant snacking during the movies, I somehow felt ravenous. Jinseung didn't eat much of his own meal, seemingly preferring to watch me eat instead.

"Not hungry?" I asked.

"Must have eaten too much popcorn."

"But it's so delicious!"

"I'll take it home and eat it later."

"Okay, suit yourself."

He continued to watch me eat for a few more minutes, head resting in his hands. "Chloe…" he said tentatively.

"Hmmm?"

"You're not going to Busan anymore, right?"

"I'm staying here."

"Then are you still looking for somewhere to live?"

"Yeah. I mean, there are a few options I could take. None of them great."

"The vacant apartment…please take it."

The offer was tempting, but it was overly generous. I didn't want to be a burden on Jinseung, nor did I want to rely on him too much. "I don't know…"

"Please. I want to help you."

His insistence was so earnest that it didn't take much to wear my resistance down. "Well…Okay. But only until I have a job."

"I'm not going to be able to convince you to stay there longer than that, am I?"

"No."

"*Aigoo*. I like your independent streak. And you're stubborn, just like me."

I checked the time. "It's after midnight."

"Should we call it a night then?"

"But I don't want to."

"Then perhaps...should we head back to my apartment?"

"Is the no-sleepover rule still in play?"

Jinseung laughed. "No. That was recently abolished."

49

Two weeks later

A pang of guilt hit me as I looked around the lavish apartment, box of belongings in hand. I wondered how much income Jinseung was sacrificing to let me live here rent-free.

Putting my feelings of guilt aside, I released the heavy box from my arms onto the living room floor. As I stood back up, I noticed a bottle of wine wrapped in purple ribbons on the dining table, a note alongside it. I unfolded the small piece of paper.

See you tonight x

It had been a little while since I last saw Jinseung and this reminder that we would shortly see each other again filled my heart with joy.

Feeling reenergised, I started to unpack my things. It didn't take long to find a place for everything in the spacious apartment. With that done, I needed to go to the supermarket to stock the pantry for the evening's meal. I grabbed my bag and headed out.

An hour later I returned, arms aching from lugging two shopping bags brimming with produce.

As I prepared dinner, my lingering sense of guilt started to be overshadowed by the satisfaction of getting to cook in a full-sized kitchen with all the bells and whistles. I turned some music on and sang at the top of my lungs while I chopped vegetables.

My singing aloud continued while the food cooked in the oven and I almost didn't hear my phone ringing. I quickly turned down the music and ran to pick up my phone on the last ring. "*Yeoboseyo?*"

"Chloe, I'm afraid I have some bad news," Jinseung said, voice sombre.

I braced myself, fearing I was about to be let down. "What's wrong?"

"...I have to cancel tonight."

There it is. "Why?" I croaked. My throat was dry and tight. *All this dinner preparation. All for nothing.*

"I'm sorry. It's work. I can't get out of it."

Before I could express my disappointment to him, the doorbell rang.

"Hold on a sec," I said. *Who's ringing the bell if it's not Jinseung?* I answered the door, bemused.

Jinseung stood outside, handsome as ever, crooked grin on his irresistibly cute face. He bore a bouquet of flowers and a box of fancy chocolates.

I gasped in outrage. "You're evil!"

"Did I take that joke too far?"

"Yes! How could you say that?"

"But aren't you relieved I'm here?"

"Incredibly relieved. But don't do something like that again!"

"All right, all right." He sniffed the air as he brought the flowers and chocolate inside. "Wow, smells delicious! What's cooking?"

"A traditional British roast. Well, as traditional as possible with the ingredients available here."

"*Daebak.*"

"I told you I would make it for you."

"I remember. Thank you." He looked around. "I like what you've done with the place."

I laughed. "It doesn't look any different. I don't have enough stuff to fill up a space as big as this. I shouldn't get too comfortable here anyway. Soon, the school will rent an apartment for me."

"So you heard back?"

"Yes. I got the job!"

He hugged me. "That's great! I knew you wouldn't struggle to find something."

"And the good news doesn't end there. Remember how I got scammed by that teaching placement company? They have been fined for their actions, so I'll be getting some compensation."

"Good. Compensation is the least you deserve for going through all that."

"It definitely helps."

"I have some good news too."

"Oh yeah? What is it?"

"My latest audition went really well, and I've already been invited back for a screen test. If I get it, it'll be my biggest role yet."

"That's amazing! It seems like you've landed back on your feet."

"A good excuse to celebrate, don't you think? Shall we crack open that bottle of wine?"

"Good idea."

He opened the bottle and poured us each a generous glass. As I drank, I mused on how far I'd come in the last few months—from the clueless girl who got scammed, to an actor in a K-drama with wonderful friends in the entertainment industry, and even a famous boyfriend who seemed to adore me. Even though I would be dropping acting for teaching soon, the future excited me.

"What are you smiling about?" Jinseung asked, lips quirked in amusement.

"Oh, I was just thinking how lucky I am."

He shook his head. "I don't believe in luck. Good things happen when you're a good person."

"That's—" Suddenly all of the lights turned off, leaving the room in darkness. "Huh? What's going on?"

"Must be a power cut." He looked out the window. "Yep. It's affecting this whole area."

I felt a surge of panic. "Oh no! What about dinner?" I rushed to open the oven. "It hasn't finished cooking."

"Hopefully it will come back on soon, but for now, let's light some candles and just enjoy it."

I sat back down, arms folded, feeling bitter about my dinner being ruined if the power didn't come back on. Meanwhile Jinseung placed some candles around the room, lit them, then pulled the throw off the couch and laid it out on the floor.

"What are you doing?" I asked.

"It's an indoor picnic. We can sit on the floor, drink some

wine, and eat some chocolate while the candles flicker around us. Isn't it kind of romantic? Come here."

Still pouting about dinner, I reluctantly joined him. He pulled me into his arms, my head leaned back on his chest.

"See, isn't this nice?" he murmured into my ear.

I had to admit, it was pretty romantic.

He began to kiss my neck, light and fluttery, mixed with his warm breath making my skin prickle. The candles glowed softly in the background. We sank low onto the floor, limbs tangled. He kissed me slowly, taking his time to draw out each glorious sensation. I was completely at his mercy.

"Chloe," he said between kisses. "Let's go public with our relationship…"

I pulled back in surprise. "Huh?"

"…In one year."

"Oh."

"If you can put up with me for that long."

The power came back on, and everything started up again with a whirr and buzz.

One year. I couldn't possibly know what would be in store for us. The only thing I knew for sure was that I was willing to put my heart on the line to be with him.

I nodded. "Okay. One year."

GLOSSARY

- **-ah/-ya** — A casual title used when addressing a close friend
- **-nim** — An honorific used when addressing someone by their profession
- **-ssi** — A polite title used when addressing someone
- **Abeoji** — Father
- **Aegyo** — A display of cutesy gestures/behaviour
- **Agassi** — Polite way to address a young unmarried female
- **Aigoo** — An exclamation expressing surprise or exasperation
- **Ajumma** — A middle-aged woman
- **Banchan** — Side dish
- **Banmal** — Informal form of Korean language
- **Bibimbap** — Korean mixed rice dish
- **Bulgogi** — Korean marinated beef or pork
- **Daebak** — Awesome
- **Dongsaeng** — Younger sibling/friend
- **Eomeoni** — Mother

- **Eomma** — Mum
- **Galbi** — Korean grilled ribs
- **Gimbap** — Korean seaweed and rice roll
- **Hagwon** — Cram school
- **Hwaiting** — An expression of encouragement
- **Hyung** — Used by males to address older brothers or older male friends
- **Jajangmyeon** — Noodles in black bean sauce
- **Jjimjilbbang** — Bathhouse / sauna
- **Kkoolbbang** — A sweet made from bean paste inside fried dough
- **Maknae** — Youngest sibling or youngest team member
- **Noona** — Used by males to address older sisters or older female friends
- **Noraebang** — Karaoke venue
- **Omo** — An expression of shock or surprise
- **Oppa** — Used by females to address their older brother, older male friends, or boyfriend
- **PD** — The director of a TV programme
- **Pojangmacha** — A street food stall in a tent
- **Ramyeon** — Ramen
- **Samgyupsal gui** — Grilled pork belly
- **Saranghae** — I love you (informal)
- **Seonbae** — Senior
- **Seonsaeng-nim** — Teacher
- **Tteokbokki** — A dish of rice cakes in a spicy sauce
- **Unnie** — Used by females to address their older sisters or older female friends
- **Yeobo** — Darling / Honey
- **Yeoboseyo** — Used when you answer the phone
- **Yo** — Traditional Korean mattress

Printed in Great Britain
by Amazon